| Moondust

MOONDUST

The Twisted Realm Series Book One

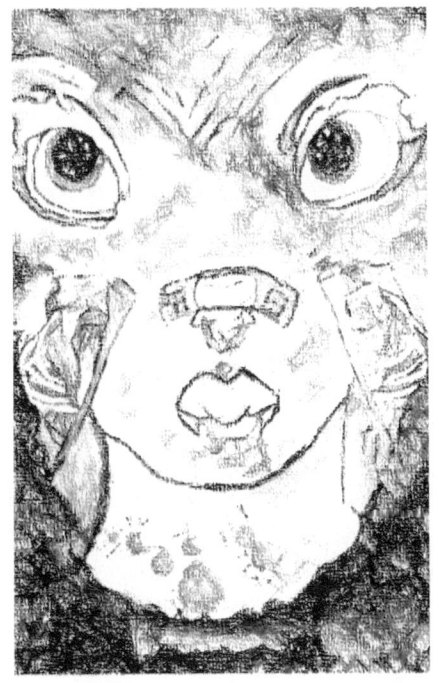

Megan Guilliams

Dark Moon Rising Publications | Virginia

Dark Moon Rising Publications

2289 Henry Rd
Ferrum, Virginia   24088
Tel: (540) 257-2861

Any and all characters are a work of fiction

Printed in the United States of America

Edited by Megan Guilliams

Cover art by Megan Guilliams

For Little Devan Junior. You are the coolest kid I know.
Thank you for being the best son in the world.

ACKNOWLEDGMENT

I want to thank my beta readers for all their demanding work and support. In no particular order

1 Ann Moschler

2 Amy Booth

3 Heather Adkins

4 Sabrina Lynch

5 Jamie Lynch

6 Bree Coleman

7 Shay Brown Doula

8 Gerald Sigmon

9 Darren Moore

10 Brittany Ashley Hairston

I also want to take a moment to give a shout-out to the best Mother and Father-in-law, a girl could honestly ask for.

We love you, Edward and Judy Guilliams. Thank you for letting us join your family <3

With Love, Megan Wright

Moondust

Andrew looked down at the girl. He would have thought she was asleep if he didn't know better. Her mahogany brown hair lay around her head like a beautiful silky halo. Her eyes were shut, but Andrew could imagine them big and brown, twinkling in childlike wonderment. Her skin was smooth and caramel, kissed by the sun that had long since set behind the man. Who could have done this? He thought to himself. She was far from the first.

Andrew Bower was the town's medical examiner and local private investigator. I know that would seem odd to most people, but it worked well for him, and the city Chairperson Howards had hired him to end the rash of teenage deaths in Finch Hollow. Zipping up the bag and putting the poor girl on the gurney, Andrew and his medical nurse wheeled her into the ambulance and let it leave for the hospital's morgue. Andrew always liked to stick around for a while and try to catch all the information he could from the local police officers. Some of them had loose lips, but most liked Andrew and wanted to help as much as possible. He was a good guy at the end of the day, and the police officers of Finch Hollow sometimes needed the extra help...

As long as he didn't get in their way.

"So, what are we looking at here?" Officer Jenkins asked another older officer.

"It would seem like we might have another suicide on our hands." He responded as he got down on one knee to look closely at the blood-splattered pavement. "She climbed the tower steps and jumped from the top. We won't know exactly when she did this until Drew returns to the hospital and gives an official statement." Andrew knew that was a nudge to get out of their way, but he lingered in the shadows long enough to catch a few more bits of information that would save him valuable time later.

"Looks like her name was Darla Snead. Her mother lives in the middle of town in that old apartment complex on West and fifth street." Jenkins muttered. "Looks like Darla had a birthday last week. She turned nineteen on the twenty-first." Andrew nodded and tipped his hat at Jenkins before getting his partner and heading for his old yellow beater. Andrew never thought to upgrade his ride. He had the funds but had, for some reason, grown quite attached to the old thing. It needed a new belt somewhere because every time Andrew started the rusty lemon, it would squeal like a banshee for about five seconds.

The drive didn't take long, maybe five minutes from where the tower was. Most people called it the tower, but it was an old steeple attached to the church on the east side of town. Every Sunday at ten in the morning, the priest would walk the steps to the top of the steeple and wake up the sleepy town and remind them to put on their best digs and roll into the church. A lot of people did too. This was a small community, and everyone here tended to be God-fearing in some capacity. Andrew wasn't so much of a church goer as a spiritual man. He rarely went to church; when he did, it was never that church. He felt this might make him less likely to favor the cloth if it came down to it.

Getting out of the old yellow car, the two of them made it to the morgue without saying a word to each other, but the minute the door closed behind them, they were bouncing questions and theories back and forth like over-caffeinated schoolgirls.

"What does that make now, Hunter? Five? Five dead teens. All of them dead at the church's doorstep in some way." Hunter nodded at Drew and put a thinking finger beside his lip.

3

"I think it's pretty obvious that if these aren't suicides, then someone or ONES have it out for the church." Andrew sat down at his desk and looked over at the dead girl, who was now disrobed and under a white sheet. She still looked asleep, and that's how he wanted to remember her. It is always a shame when someone that young dies, but it's a downright tragedy when it repeatedly happens in a few weeks.

"So, you're convinced that the church had nothing to do with it?"

"I doubt the church would kill children and lay them on their doorstep like that... No, Drew, I've counted the cloth out of this one... at least for now." Andrew tended to agree with his partner for the time being. Pulling out his files, he rummaged around until he found the four, he was looking for.

"The first of them was Gary Wilson. He was eighteen. Hung himself in the dining hall with an extension cord. No recent birthday, no family trauma... Good kid. I had to rule this one a suicide. The only marks on him were from the cord. I went over and over this one. What triggered the others?" Hunter shrugged his shoulders and walked over to the girl on the slab.

"While you go over those files for the millionth time, I'm going to take Darla's liver temp. Maybe a time of death would help us out here." Andrew nodded at Hunter and opened the second file.

"Then there was Marybelle Lancaster... She drowned herself in the baptism pool four days later... simple drowning, no foul play. She was nineteen, shy, and reserved. Marybelle went to church every Sunday with her aunt. She was almost twenty. She would have had a birthday in like six weeks." Hunter pulled the thermometer out of its cleaning solution and put on his blue rubber gloves. He wasn't as nearly interested in the old information as the new. Pushing the rod through Darla's side and puncturing her liver, he waited for the results.

"Fifty-five degrees on a crisp September day... that doesn't seem right to me. There's no way she was out there that long without being noticed. What do you think, Drew?" Hunter turned around to face his friend, who hadn't heard the question. He was still nose deep in the files once again.

"Susan Waller, seventeen. Slit her wrists while sitting in one of the pews. She was outgoing and popular and didn't have a care in the world. Her mother even told me she had made some early college admissions. That doesn't sound like the actions of a girl who would just up and kill herself." Hunter couldn't help but roll his eyes at the man. He was nothing if not meticulous; he would give Drew that much.

"Drew," Hunter began again but was cut short when he turned to face Darla's body. He couldn't quite believe what he was seeing and instinctually pulled the thermometer from the girls' side and
5

stepped away. "Andrew, what... was that there before?" He could answer his question; he couldn't understand the logic of it. As Andrew continued down the rabbit hole, he could see the marks forming right in front of his eyes.

"Then there was George Conner. Age eighteen, two days ago. He jumped off the church roof. George was the only one out of the bunch who had apparently had some drug issues. Maybe he was high when he fell, and we might never know, mostly because the family refused an autopsy and had him cremated. What do all these kids have in common, Hunter... What are we missing? Hunter?" His friend's lack of response made him turn around in curiosity. What he saw made his eyes widen. "Did you do that to the body for some reason?" Drew asked, and Hunter shook his head no. Slack-jawed Hunter continued to back away slowly with the thermometer in one hand and the other in a white-knuckled fist. Drew, on the other hand, walked toward the body in wonderment. It looked like a symbol had emerged from the girl's chest between the collarbones—four small spirals. Andrew reached out and pulled the sheet down a little to look just in time for Darla's eyes to flutter open, and a loud shrill cry escaped her lips. Grabbing the sheet, she sat up quickly on the slab and wrapped the sheet tight around herself.

"What the Hell is going on?" She shrieked as Drew backed away from the girl's hands in the air.

"I honestly have no idea," Andrew began.

6

"Yeah," Hunter said, "I've been at this for a while now, and I've never seen a dead one come back to life before. Does that mean we are really good or bad at our jobs?"

"Ha-ha, hilarious, guys," Darla began. "I want to go home. Where are we, and what have you done with my clothes?"

"Chances are they cut them off of you when they brought you to the morgue. I can probably find you some scrubs, though," Hunter said in a rushed tone and ran out of the door. There was a stunned silence in the room. Drew didn't know where to begin as he looked at the girl in awe and maybe just a little fear. Finally, he spoke.

"I can't believe that you're up and walking around. You were dead just a few minutes ago." Andrew took a step closer, and Darla instinctively scooted further back.

"Well, clearly, I'm not dead."

"I don't know, Darla... You couldn't have possibly survived that fall." Darla looked the man over and squinted her eyes.

"Well then, are you dead too?"

"I doubt it," Drew responded as he walked back to the desk and picked up the folders. He was sliding them back into the filing cabinet.

"Are you sure?" Darla asked, and Drew began to respond but quickly shut his mouth and scratched his head. Hunter fumbled down the hallway, scrubs in hand, when he passed Kelly going in the opposite direction.

"Hey there, buddy! Where are you going in such a hurry?" Hunter gave her an awkward smile.

"Umm, there was an accident in the morgue. Andrew needs scrubs." Hunter only paused for a moment before rushing past her.

"Eww, don't tell me anything else about that." She said as she continued to the steps leading to the emergency room. Hunter didn't give this anymore thought until later. Kelly should have never been in the basement; she should have never been there at all.

Once Darla had gotten dressed, and Andrew had convinced her that they weren't crazy people, she allowed them to give her an exam. Sitting in the rolling chair by the desk, Darla looked at the two of them as they looked down at her instead of her smashed head.

"This is absolutely fascinating," Drew muttered as he took a gloved hand and gingerly touched the wound. "Can you feel that?"

"What? Are you touching my head? Yes." Darla muttered, and Drew didn't have to look at her face to know that she was rolling her eyes.

"And it doesn't hurt?" Hunter asked in astonishment. "Does that mean that it's dead tissue?"

"I honestly have no idea; this is the first time I've ever encountered anything like this. It's so... Fascinating." He said again. "I can see grey matter and bone fragments; there's little to no blood or fluids of any kind surrounding the wound. If she weren't up and walking around, I would have to say she was deceased."

"And yet here I am, a walking talking person, probably with a concussion or something, but I'm certainly not dead."

"I wouldn't be so sure about that. When I took Darla's liver temperature, it was at fifty-five degrees which would have implicated that she had been dead for more than a day. It's the first suicide attempt in weeks that doesn't match up with the crime scene." Hunter looked over at Andrew as the realization hit him. Eyes wide, he rolled the girl around and lifted the bottom of her scrubs to reveal a large hole in her side.

"You took her liver temp?" Andrew asked. The look of astonishment grew even more apparent. Darla looked down at the wound on her side.

"What the hell did you do to me?" She shrieked.

"There is absolutely no way you're alive, Darla! You have a large hole in your liver. You wouldn't be able to sustain function. You would be in renal failure at the very least." Darla looked over at Drew and

9

scowled, "What am I then, doctor?" Andrew shrugged his shoulders and knelt beside her in the chair.

"I'm going to try to find out for you. You'll have to trust me, though, right?" Darla didn't feel like she had much choice. Reluctantly, she nodded, and Andrew got to his feet in rushed excitement. Grabbing a pad and a pen from the desk, Andrew jumped up on the slab and sat down.

"What do you remember from the last day you were, um, not hurt." Taking a deep breath, Darla closed her eyes and tried to think back. Back to the last thing she could remember before waking up in the morgue.

"I was walking, and I'm sure I was going to the library. Something told me to go to the church... It was right down the road from where I was going anyway. Please don't ask me why I wanted to go there. I rarely want to go on Sundays. My mom makes me anyway. She would always say that dumb old cliched My house. My rules crap if I put up a fight about it. I think we fought earlier that day as well. I remember being angry at her for something... Yes! I remember now I was going to the library to use the computer. I was going house hunting. Time to leave the nest, so to speak." Darla let out a little snort. Hunter could tell she was really into the memory; neither of the men interrupted her as she continued. "I still don't know why I went to the church, though; I was probably about on the third flight of steps before I stopped myself, or someone stopped me... That part is a little foggy. I remember hearing my mother's voice."

"Was she there with you at the church?" Hunter asked. This was the first, and probably the last, time Hunter would ever be able to question a murder victim, and for some reason, that excited him.

"No," Darla began again. "She wasn't there with me; it was almost like she was... I don't know, like in my head or something. She told me to stop, like she knew something bad would happen to me. Whatever it was, it made me turn around and start walking back down the stairs. I remember Father Hall at the bottom of the steps. He didn't ask me what I was doing on the steeple. He didn't seem surprised that a random girl was wandering around the place on a Tuesday morning."

"Wait a minute," Hunter said, putting a hand in the air. "Tuesday morning? The last memory you've had was on a Tuesday." Darla opened her eyes so that she could roll them at the man.

"Yes, brilliant deduction. You must be the best detective in all of Finch Hollow." Her sarcasm wasn't lost on Hunter. He couldn't help but smirk at her before continuing with his reasoning.

"I was going to say that you've been... Asleep for quite a while then; today is Friday." Darla gave the man a weird look.

"There's no way I missed three days somewhere. What could I have been doing for that long...? My mom would have put out a missing person thing, and my friends would have been looking for me." Andrew, who had been fervently writing down everything Darla had been saying, finally took a break and looked over at the girl.

"Everything you said is probably accurate. I didn't get to meet you until tonight, and with all the commotion, I haven't been able to get more information on you than your name and where you used to live. It would make sense that Jenkins had even that much information due to a missing person's report. Keep going, Darla. You're doing great. Do you remember anything else?" Darla closed her eyes once again and thought for a moment before continuing.

"I remember walking out of the church, wondering why it was already dark outside. I couldn't have been in there that long. I remember a bright light rushing up on me and a loud bang, then... Nothing." Darla opened her eyes to see the two men looking at each other, perplexed at the story, trying to make sense of everything that had happened tonight.

"Well, one thing for sure, she can't go home." Hunter blurted out.

"Why not!" Darla protested, but Hunter put a quieting hand in the air, and she quickly shut her mouth.

"Darla, look at yourself; you're not exactly at a hundred percent; we don't know if you're going to heal yourself or not, we don't know how your mother is going to react, and we certainly don't know if your life is still in danger. Putting you in the open with your mother could put you and her in danger." Darla wanted to protest, but she couldn't think of a valid argument that would trump his.

"Fine then," Andrew said as he jumped off the slab. "We shouldn't let you out of our sights either. You can come to stay with me." Again, Hunter put a hand in the air.

"I have a better idea; why don't the two of you stay with me? I have an extra room, and your apartment is small and crowded. I wouldn't want people to see her, especially people who might know her mother or her friends." Andrew nodded in approval as the three devised a plan to get her to the car.

It was three in the morning when Hannah woke up from a rather horrible nightmare. She knew this fact for sure when she picked up her digital clock and looked at its face. Hannah had had these dreams increasingly and more frequently since she had done that ceremony with Darla's mother. If given a chance, she wouldn't have done it again, but at the time, she felt like she had no other choice. Her friend was missing, and Darla's mother was beside herself with worry. Looking down at her bandaged hand, she carefully unwrapped it to expose her wound. For some reason, it still didn't look like it was even beginning to heal. It would weep heavily if she tried to put pressure on it. It was a simple ceremony, fashion a spiral made of metal and hold it in your hand... She, Darla's mother, Matt, and Will. They all did this. Will was Darla's boyfriend, and he would have done anything to have her back in his life, even if it meant standing in the middle of her living room with a silly ass paperclip in his right-hand chanting some made-up language. At the same time, Darla's mother, Claire, threw rose petals and herbs in the air like a weirdo hippy.

At first, nothing happened. Hannah thought that Claire would have a fit, but then he saw the look of pain on Matt's face first. Will wasn't far behind, looking down at his hand... Then Hannah. It was a warm feeling and then burning. The metal in their hands was burning the symbol into their palms, and no matter how much they tried to drop it, the spiral embedded more profoundly into their flesh until nothing was left of the metal spiral. No one said anything afterward. They all just went home and tried to forget what had happened. Hannah couldn't bring herself back to Claire's and check on things. What if the ceremony didn't work, or worse yet, what if it had?

Rolling over in her bed, she closed her eyes and tried to go back to sleep, but the memory of that horror-filled nightmare crept back into her head. It always started the same way. She wakes up in her bed, and the sun is out. Hannah could see that she had left her window open the night before because the pink lace curtains framing it began to blow in the crisp fall breeze. The dream was so absolute that she could feel the wind kissing her blushed cheeks. A strand of blond hair always falls over her blue eyes, and Hannah brushed it away absently, getting out of bed and walking to the window to shut it. Looking back on this simple part of the dream, Hannah is convinced that if her hair hadn't obstructed her vision, she might have noticed the footprints in her white plush carpet earlier.

As most youngsters do, she makes her way out of the bedroom and down the hall. This is where Hannah would see the first thing that makes her pause and realize that she is, once again, in a dream. The bloody handprint at the end of the hall. The first two or three times she had this dream, she would cautiously walk down and turn to the kitchen, where she would always meet with carnage. Her mother and father were murdered in cold blood. Her brother was decapitated, his head on a platter in the middle of the kitchen table like a fine thanksgiving turkey. She refused to go to the kitchen the second to last time, only to be met with a masked assailant in her closet. He would bum-rush her with a bloody butcher knife. She woke up right before the blade would have been plunged into her heart. Tonight though was the worst. She woke up in her room just the same as every other nightmare she's had for the last week. She knew better than to stay in her room. She took a deep breath and walked down the hall, but the bloody handprint wasn't there. Hoping against hope, she wouldn't be met with carnage, Hannah turned the corner to the

16

kitchen. All hope had vanished when she saw the same gory horror show. Putting a hand on the hallway wall, Hannah felt something sticky and quickly took her hand away. Looking down, she saw the bloody handprint... it was hers, and to her horror, on the other hand, was the bloody knife used by the killer himself. Hannah knew in a heartbeat that she had killed them all. Was she the monster? Was she a killer? NO! She didn't want to think about that, not tonight. Not ever.

The sun began to rise when Hannah's eyes fluttered open for the second time. Something didn't feel quite the same as every other morning. Swinging her feet to the floor, she noticed the window over her writing desk had been left open. The pink lace curtains flowed on the crisp September morning. A ray of sunlight reflected on the blue binder she had put on the table after school. She had forgotten to put it back in her backpack. A wisp of blond hair fell across her face as she stood up to shut the window. She didn't like the feeling of Deja vu. It was like she was inside her dream, but this was real life. Slamming the window shut, Hannah picked up her folder and turned toward her closet. She had thrown her backpack in there after school. Her nerves were raw, and her knees shook as she stepped towards the door. Reaching a handout, she felt the cold steel of the closet door between her fingers. Taking a deep breath, she turned the knob and flung the door open. She was fully prepared for the attack, but nothing came. She reached out another hand and began moving the

17

clothes around in the closet, but there was no one inside the cabinet.

Hannah let out a little laugh as she reached down, snatching her bag and sliding the folder inside of it. Hannah shut the closet door, put her backpack on her bed, and walked down the hall. She could smell breakfast on the stove. She waited for her mother's voice to call out, for her bother to threaten to eat the last strip of bacon. The rustle of her father's newspaper, but nothing came from the kitchen... Nothing but the smell of freshly brewed coffee and the skillet sizzle.

Hannah's sense of dread returned as she made her way down the hall, letting her fingers run down the length of the wall until the end. There she stopped right before turning the corner and making her entrance into the kitchen.

"Hey, guys?" Hannah asked meekly, "You in there? Breakfast smells great." Still, no one responded to her. She held her breath as she finally mustered up the courage to face what was in her kitchen. Like in her dream, her parents were sitting across from each other. Both of their throats were slit ear to ear. They were staring lifelessly at the ceiling, and the blood had soaked the white tablecloth a dark, brooding shade of crimson. Her brother was at the front of the table, his head completely removed from his neck and placed on a giant dinner plate in the center.

Hannah tried to scream, but nothing came out. Falling to the floor, she began to sob, and that's when she saw for the first time that her feet were also soaked in the same dark crimson blood as the tablecloth. She couldn't believe it. There was just no way that her feet could be soaked in her parents' blood. She never even walked into the kitchen.

Mustering up all she could, Hannah rose to her feet and looked back down the hallway, and there, like magic, was a long streak of blood where she had run her fingers down the wall... and in her left hand was the blade.

Hunter didn't get much sleep that night, and after breakfast, he offered to stay with Darla while Andrew went to see Darla's mother. Darla didn't seem to be a threat, but Hunter was an avid horror movie fan and had seen almost every zombie flick imaginable. It was just a matter of time before she began to do something out of the realm of normal. Hunter could feel it in his bones. He didn't want to be caught off guard.

He had watched her for most of the night. He didn't want to come off as a weirdo, but he also didn't want to be attacked in his sleep... One thing was for sure, and she didn't sleep, not even a cat nap the whole time he had eyes on her; this morning, she didn't eat a single thing. No, Hunter knew that this wouldn't end well for them. Not unless he kept a close eye on their little zombie girl.

It didn't take long to reach Darla's mother's apartment. It was the biggest one in the whole town and the oldest. Andrew had never been inside the place, but he was in awe of its sheer size. He knew you had to have quite a bit of money even to be considered for a lease in this place. Pushing the buzzer to Claire's apartment, he could hear the woman's voice through the intercom.

"Yes, can I help you?" The voice sounded almost identical to that of Darla's. Andrew didn't know why he was surprised by that; Claire was, after all, Darla's mother.

"Claire? Andrew, the medical examiner of Finch Hollow, and I just wanted to ask you a few questions about your daughter." There was a long silence before he heard the loud beep of the door opening. Walking inside, he had to take everything in before making his way to her door. The inside was just as impressive as the outside—high ceilings with a hanging chandelier right in the center. A doorman at the front desk was wearing an old bellboy's getup. He tilted his hat, and Andrew did the same as he strolled to the staircase.

Door 206, this was it. He lifted his hand to knock, but the woman opened the door, and their eyes met for the first time. Andrew had lived here most of his life, but he was more than sure he had never seen Claire before this day. She was very much like her daughter. She was slim and feminine, with long, flowing black hair and the same caramel sun-kissed skin. She had large almond-shaped eyes that twinkled in the hallway light, almost as if they were filled with glitter. They might have been the most beautiful shade of brown Andrew had ever seen.

"Well, are you going to come in, or are you going to gawk at me from the hallway?" Claire asked with a bit of tilt of her head. Andrew blinked his eyes a few times and then nodded. With a smile, he walked past her into the apartment, and she shut the door behind them.

Motioning for him to sit on the couch, he did as he was told, and Claire decided to sit in the high-backed chair across from him.

"I don't know what other information I can give you that I haven't already given the police," Claire said quickly. Andrew took off his fedora before proceeding with his questions. This place made him feel he needed to be a little more formal than average.

"Ms...." Andrew was cut off by a hand in the air. "Please," Claire began, "You can call me Claire. All of Darla's friends do... Did." Claire looked at the floor. Andrew could tell that she was still getting over her daughter's death. It had only been a few days.

"Okay then, Claire, I want to know what you remember from when she vanished. Did you two argue? Did she have any enemies?" Claire nodded and crossed her legs.

"I know you dabble at being a private investigator, and an elected official has hired you to find out why there has been a rash of teen deaths in the last few weeks. I know this elected official quite well, so I will tell you a little story... One that I didn't bother to tell the police because I don't think they would have used the information wisely."

Claire gave the man a once over before continuing with her story. He seemed to be on the up and up, which was a breath of fresh air for the likes of Claire. He was a tall, broad-shouldered man with a wisp of brown, curly hair on the top of his head. He wore a fedora most days to hide the widow's peak that gave away his age. He had frown lines on his cheeks and worry lines across his forehead, but on either side of his thin lips was just a hint of laugh lines. Yes, this man had lived a life full of emotion. Claire thought that if anyone could make sense of what she was going to say, it would be him.

"I'm not sure if you know the history of this small town. I'm not talking about the founder and the first building; I'm talking about the little colony that settled here before the land was cultivated nearly four hundred years ago. I know this will sound little nuts but hear me out." Andrew nodded. The last thing he had planned to do was stop this woman from speaking her peace. Listening was one of the things this man could do well, and he did it often and at great length.

"There were probably no more than five hundred or so settlers here in Finch Hollow, but back then, it was known as Fischer's Bay. Most of the town's men were anglers and did well the first year they were here. When the second spring came, another smaller colony set up camp on the other side of the lake. This colony brought foreign illnesses. Some said the plague, and some said scarlet fever. Honestly, I don't think the illness itself matters at this point. It wiped out almost everyone in the town. As the last of the settlers began to show signs of this horrible disease, the colonies' priest crossed the lake to confront the group. Possibly to ask for help, some said he was delirious from fever; whatever the case, the priest never returned. Now here's the kicker...." Claire leaned in for dramatic effect, and Andrew did so in turn.

"It was said that the smaller colony was a tight-knit group of people consisting of only five families, and the nuns from the fallen priest began to curse their names. I doubt that the nuns knew the names of those people... Unfortunately, neither do I, but what I do know is the name of the second smaller group. Maynor's Wisp. If you look into this group, you might find a connection to the kids."

Andrew's eyes widened as he got to his feet.

"Ms. Snead, I believe you might have cracked this thing wide open for me." Claire smiled a little and nodded her head. She knew what she had done, and he had taken the bait precisely as he was supposed to.

24

Claire was a damn good judge of character and was yet to be let down. Getting to her feet, she showed the man to the door.

"Please, call me Claire, and if you have more questions, you know where to find me." Andrew shook the ladies' hand before making his way to the front door of the apartment complex, the door man was nowhere to be seen on the way out, but Andrew paid that no mind. He was on his way to the local library. He had so much to think about, but Claire had opened the door of opportunity, and Andrew wasn't the one to pass that up.

Hunter had been sitting on the couch for a few hours and had haphazardly turned on the television. Darla was in the kitchen. He thought he had heard the refrigerator door open and shut a few times; he hadn't supposed anything of it. Finally, Hunter got to his feet. He knew he should be watching the girl, but a wave of sleepiness put him back on the couch. Hunter could feel his eyes flutter shut. This was it, he thought; this is how I get bit. That was not the case; this was the evening he rested well. With Darla otherwise preoccupied in the kitchen doing God knows what and Andrew waist-deep at the library on a hunch, the house was almost dead silent, save for the tv in the background. When he finally woke up, it was the sound of the phone ringing off the hook. Waking with a start, Hunter fell off the couch, and he could hear Darla giggling from the next room.

"It's been ringing for a while now, but I didn't want to answer. Too many questions as to who I might be." Hunter didn't have any problem with her not answering the phone. He had told Drew they needed to buy another answering machine, but they had both forgotten after the rash of deaths around town. Getting to his feet, Hunter looked over at Darla, who had a pudding pop in her mouth. He could tell that the girl had had more than her fair share while he was asleep. He didn't know whether to be happy or concerned.

"After I find out who's on the other line, I'll check out your head again. Hopefully, there are some signs of improvement. After all, it does look like you've found your appetite. I'm hoping that's a good thing." Darla nodded in approval and returned to the kitchen, where he heard the refrigerator door open again. Hunter grabbed the phone from the table beside the couch and cleared his throat.

"William's residence; this is Hunter speaking."

"Hunter? Have you seen Andrew?" A familiar voice was on the other side of the line, and it took Hunter a moment to realize to whom he was talking.

"Oh, officer Jenkins, I'm sorry I haven't heard from him in a while." Looking over at the wall clock beside the kitchen door, Hunter only realized what time it was. "Oh, scratch that... I haven't heard from him in over three hours. Is there anything I can help you with?" There was a long pause on the other line before the police officer decided whether to continue.

"I wouldn't bother you if it weren't a matter of urgency, Mr. Williams, but we have a... Situation." There was another long pause before Jenkins continued. He could hear the uneasiness in his voice, and it didn't do anything to calm Hunter's nerves.

"Look, I know I'm not Andrew, but I've been doing this with him for the last five years. I used to live in a bigger city than this doing the same thing, so I assure you that you're in good hands... Even if they are unfamiliar ones." This seemed to calm the policeman's nerves enough to continue his explanation of what had happened.

"Mr. Williams, as I said before, I wouldn't have bothered you if this weren't a time-sensitive matter, and as much as we have tried to get ahold of Andrew, we had no luck. He must have forgotten to charge his cell."

"Or left it in the car," Hunter muttered as he rolled his eyes. Andrew was nothing if not forgetful when it came to his cell phone. He had only had it a few months, and he thought of them about as fondly as an electronic leash. Hunter wasn't sure if the man had forgotten the phone or didn't want people to know where he was. Either way, it wasn't very pleasant.

"Either way, this situation has three bodies. Hannah Whitcomb is our prime suspect." Hunter's eyes began to widen as the realization hit him.

Hannah was a friend of his. He used to tutor her when he first moved to town. She was fourteen, fresh-faced, and ready for the trials of high school. Her mother was an overachiever and wanted her daughter to have a little extra edge walking into the anatomy hall on her first day. She had initially asked Andrew to do it, but he couldn't, seeing as he was working on something outside of town. He had never had someone he knew pass like this before, and certainly not at her daughter's hands.

"Has she said anything to you?" Hunter asked. He could hear Darla wandering out of the kitchen again, this time with what looked like a turkey on whole wheat.

"Hey Hunter, when you get off the phone, I wanna watch some tv. You're running out of food." Putting his hand over the mouthpiece, Hunter gave the girl a little look but dialed it back a notch when he took a good look at her face. Her eyes looked bloodshot, almost as if she were food drunk. Mustering as much positivity as he could, he smiled and nodded.

"Just a minute more," Hunter whispered. With an exasperated sigh, she plopped on the couch and looked for the remote.

"Mr. Williams, that's just the thing. She's said many things, but we aren't sure if it makes any sense. We took her to the hospital and had her checked out. Everything seems normal, but the CT scan hasn't come back. We can't rule out brain trauma of some kind."

"Have we received the bodies?" Hunter asked, tapping his finger on the table beside the old phone.

"Yes, about an hour ago. We would like for you to give them a look over and give us any information that might be useful to this case. Honestly, I can't imagine Hannah doing something like this. I don't think she has it in her." Hunter ran a hand through his hair and took another deep breath.

"I have a few things to finish here, give me an hour, and I will go the morgue and take a look. In the meantime, if you could please keep trying to contact Andrew, that would be great."

"Sure, no problem. Thank you, Mr. Williams; I know you don't know us very well, but I have every faith you can help." There was a click on the other side of the line, and Hunter rested the receiver onto the phone's cradle as he looked at Darla. Sitting beside the sofa, he tried to give her a once over. Her hair was greasy, not that it was all that great from the beginning, but it was starting to thin, especially in the areas of the trauma. Her eyes were bloodshot, and her lips were now grey. The only lips he had seen that color were on a corpse. Darla had finally found the remote and lost all interest in the sandwich she had parked in the unoccupied cushion on the other side of her.

"Darla, if we find something super cool on tv, will you sit and watch it for a little while so I can go to work? I promise to bring you back something extra delicious to eat." At the sound of food, Darla's eyes lit up again.

"I want a cheeseburger; make it bloody." Hunter nodded, even though her response made him shiver a little.

Andrew had spent most of the day at the library, burying his head in archived history books about the old town. He couldn't find anything about the two colonies or the people that made them up. It was around six when he was about to call it a night but was cut short at the library doors by an old familiar voice from the past.

"Couldn't help but notice what you were doing back there. It made me wonder if you found what you were looking for." Andrew couldn't help but smile at the woman's voice. Turning around to face the tall lady, he put a hand on his hip and tipped his hat.

"No, Zelda, unfortunately, I didn't."

"Does it have anything to do with what happened at the church lately?" Zelda always looked as if she had a shifty eye and knew more than she did. It took Andrew a while before he realized she used it to her advantage when asking questions. You see, she worked for the Finch Newspaper, which in this day and age was more of a website than a paper. He had to be careful of what he said, or she would put it on the site for everyone to read about in hours.

"Well, love, I can't comment on an ongoing investigation." Zelda blushed and put a hand to her cheek but quickly put it back down. "No, I have a very personal and passionate interest in this town's history. I was particularly interested in the 1600s today, but it doesn't look like this place's records go back that far."

"Well, I'm going home for the evening, but if you're interested in the land before it became Finch Hollow, you should talk to Mark Randolph."

"Mark Randolph? I'm not sure if I've ever heard of him." Andrew said, lifting an eyebrow. Zelda let out a little laugh and flipped her hair over her shoulder. Andrew knew this woman had always had a bit of a thing for him, and he used that to his advantage. Leaning into her, he gave her one of the best smiles he could muster and looked her in the eyes.

"Whatever happened to that dinner you promised me good-looking?" Zelda couldn't stop blushing and turned her eyes away from the man. Shifting her weight from one foot to the other, she settled her eyes on the floor.

"I mean, I might be free this weekend. Give me a call?"

"Doll. So, who is this Mark fellow you've mentioned?"

"Oh!" Zelda began and opened her folder to pull out a business card. "He lives a way out there, but he's the best damn historian and wildlife expert I've ever met. We were at this convention at Eagles Nest for a story a few months back, and I interviewed him. It would be him if anyone could get you the needed information." Taking the card from Zelda's hand, Andrew's smile widened.

"You know what, Zelda; you are one of a kind." As he walked away, he could hear the poor girl swooning. Maybe he should give her a call sometime. He hadn't been out in ages, and it would do him good to have a homecooked meal.

Getting into his car, he turned the key in the ignition, it took a few tries, but he finally got it and started hearing the old girl screech to life. Just as he was about to drive off, he noticed the icon bar on his phone had lit up. Eight missed calls, all from the same number. That couldn't be good. Unlocking the phone, he listened to the first message.

"Hey Doc, it's Officer Jenkins. We have an incident at the Whitcomb residence. If you could meet

33

us over here, that would be great." All the others were the same, and Drew knew that if he didn't get over there soon, the crime scene would be empty, and he wouldn't get in on the ground floor of what happened. Making a U-turn in the middle of the street, he floored the gas for the twenty-minute drive to the Whitcomb house.

Matt woke up from a deep sleep. He didn't know what it was that jarred him from slumber. Most of the time, it was just a loud car alarm or a police siren. He didn't live on the best side of town, but he was close enough to enjoy attending the best school. That's why his father had chosen this house from all the others in his price range when they moved here two years ago. There was... something making him feel a little nervous, but he couldn't make out exactly what it was.

After the visit with Darla's mother, Hannah and Will had been distant from him, and it sucked because they were his closest friends. He expected it from Will; Hell, he lost the love of his life; but Hannah had no reason. Thinking back to that night, he knew something weird had gone on, but he couldn't for the life of him remember. Darla's mother was unconventional... that much he could remember, but who wouldn't be after losing a kid.

Flopping back in bed, Matt put one hand over his face and tried to convince himself to go back to sleep, and it would have worked too if he hadn't heard it... The noise, he was sure, had woken him up minutes earlier. It was a rustling from the corner of his room. Sitting up again, Matt ran his hand through his long hair, trying to see into the darkness. It wasn't doing him any favors, so he reached over to turn on the bedside lamp but was met with a gloved hand instead. Opening his mouth to let out a yell, the assailant put his other hand over his mouth. His eyes widened when he realized that the hand on his face also contained a rather sharp and shiny butcher's knife.

"Look, the voice began, we don't want to hurt you. We want your hand." Two things ran through the boy's mind after he heard the burglar's comment. The word We and that this nutjob wanted to cut off his hand. Screaming through the muffled cotton glove, Matt began to kick and swing with all of his might, managing to swat the bedside lamp against the wall making a rather loud bang. Falling on its side, the circular light rolled across the table and fell onto the wooden floor with a thud.

"Stop struggling!" The masked intruder demanded as it climbed into the bed with Matt and sat on his legs, restricting the poor boy's retaliation.

Almost like magic, the lamp on the floor came to life, flooding the bedroom with enough light for Matt to count two more masked monsters. Squeezing his eyes shut, a warm salty tear ran down the boy's cheek. There was no way he could fight off three of them.

'Please,' Matt thought, 'Please let this be over.' Almost as if his prayers were being answered, he heard his father walking in from down the hall.

"Matt, I'm home, and don't even begin to tell me how you were asleep because I saw the light in your room from the window when I got out of the car." Matt's father put down his bag by the door and walked into the living room. It didn't bother him that Matt hadn't responded. He often ignored his father when he had to work late, which was most nights now that his coworker's son had passed away in the church a few weeks ago.

Johnathan Wilson had decided to take the month off to get his affairs in order. Matt's father wouldn't have blamed him if he didn't come back at all. Hell, if his son had died, he might pack up everything and moved out of the state to start over. Everything would remind him of Matt. That's no way to live. Making his way to the kitchen, Matt's father opened the freezer looking for a midnight snack, and sure enough, there was a pint of double chocolate ice cream sitting right out in front.

"This should get him down here pretty quick," Davis said as he pulled the ice cream out from the freezer and shut the door. "Yo, Matt! Let's have chocolate ice cream before we call it a night!" Davis yelled up, but again there was no answer to his call. This time he looked up at the ceiling. He could hear someone up there walking around, but his son wouldn't respond, which alarmed him. Putting the ice cream on the counter, Davis made his way back into the living room and headed towards the steps leading to the second floor. Opening the door by the kitchen door on his way over, Davis retrieved a baseball bat that had been long forgotten behind a half dozen raincoats and old work boots. When he was little, Matt used to love playing tee ball with his friends after school. Sometimes Davis wished he were still small. He sometimes felt unwanted and unneeded now. It was only a matter of months before Matt's eighteenth birthday, and Davis had no delusions that Matt wanted to stay around this town for college. It was all ending, and Davis knew it. Soon enough, he would be alone in this big house with nothing but photos to remember his son.

Creeping up the steps with as much stealth as he could, Davis held the bat with both hands, ready to strike. Matt's door was slightly ajar, and Davis thought that was weird since the hallway light always bothered him when he tried to sleep. On this occasion, though, the light was off, and when Davis reached the last step and tried to flip the switch, nothing happened. He was going in almost blind, all except for the faint tilted light coming from the crack in Matt's bedroom door. Taking a deep breath, Matt's father continued walking the four feet to his son's room, but before he could reach the handle, his feet stepped on something that made a loud cracking sound, and Davis knew right away what it was... The hallway lightbulb. If there was any doubt in his mind, it had vanished now. Someone was in there with his son, and he would stop at nothing to save him. Letting out a battle cry, Davis kicked the door open with his steel-toed boot and swung for the fences, knocking one of the masked assailants squarely in the temple, dropping them like a sack of potatoes. The other one was climbing out of the window. When this one saw Matt's father coming at them, hate raging inside and a fire in his eyes, he let go of the ledge and took the tumble off the roof.

Stopping in astonishment, Davis lowered the bat. Cocking his head to one side, he looked over at his son. He could tell that the boy had been physically shaken.

"You, okay?" Davis asked; Matt's eyes darted around the room. They were wide and squirrely, almost like a wild animal.

"D...dad..." Matt whispered and cocked his head back in a motion for Davis to come closer.

"What is it?" Davis asked as he took a few steps toward the boy. His grip on the bat tightened again. He had a feeling he was going to need it.

"There, there were three of them." Davis nodded at the boy and looked around the room. They seemed to be the only ones in there save for sleeping beauty, who had started to bleed all over the wooden floor.

"Did you see where he went?" Davis asked; Matt pulled his hand out from under the blanket and pointed to the bedroom door.

"He went into the hallway when you yelled up the first time. I don't know if he left or not." Davis' eyes widened as he saw the open gaping hole in his son's hand.

"Oh my god! What happened to you?" Matt shrugged his shoulders and quickly put his hand back under the blanket. "You need to go to the hospital! That's for sure going to need stitches."

"DAD!" Matt said in a loud whisper, "We need to focus on the task at hand. Where did this creep go?" Nodding, Davis edged his way back to the bedroom door and carefully popped his head out. If only he had a flashlight or a lighter, something that would make the hallway light up enough to make at least the shadows dance. These people were dressed all in black and would be impossible to see before it was too late. Matt summoned up all the courage he could and ventured from his bed. Grabbing a bandana from his bedside table, Matt made a bandage to keep pressure on the wound.

It was odd what had happened. One of the intruders held the boy down and covered his mouth while the other cut a quarter-sized hole out of his palm. It hurt like hell, but, for some reason, the memories of that night began to flood back... What Claire had done, and what the spell had done to his hand. But why? What purpose would that spell have if her daughter had still died? Why? It couldn't have played out as he remembered...

Making it to the door, Matt popped his head out into the hallway. He could see his father making his way to the room at the end of the hall. That room used to be his grandmother's before she passed away. She was such an avid churchgoer. Matt was never much for organized religion until his grandmother came to live with them; now, he goes every Sunday. It reminded him of Pearl; in some way, he liked to think that his grandmother looked down on him when he was in that church. Matt could barely make out his father's silhouette, but out of the corner of his eye, he could make a slight movement at the end of the hallway, directly across from the door.

"DAD!" Matt yelled as loud as he could, and his father swung around, bat first, but the masked monster managed to dodge the polished wooden Malott.

"Who the fuck ARE you!" Davis screamed as he swung at the intruder repeatedly, the burglar barely dodging impact. Pulling a knife from his belt, the faceless assailant began to turn at Matt's father in retaliation.

"All you had to do was stay at work another hour, and we would have been gone long before you got home! We had to do what we did! We saved your son's life!"

"Save his life??" Davis yelled as he swung his bat with conviction, "You put a fucking HOLE in him!" This time the bat contacted the intruder's shoulder, almost knocking it to the ground. The shadow person lunged at Davis, letting out a howl of pain, plunging its blade deep into his gut.

"That's what you get! You shouldn't have come home early!" Ripping the blade from Davis' stomach, the burglar got to his feet and ran down the steps. Matt ran to his father's side as Davis slid down the wall beside Pearl's old bedroom.

"Oh no! Dad! I'm going to get to the phone, and I'm going to call the police and an ambulance. Please, please hang in there." Davis had almost wholly lost consciousness when he hit the floor. Getting to his feet, Matt heard the front door open and close and the sound of a car racing off into the night. Running back into his room, he looked to the floor. The person, his father, who had been hit with the bat, had also vanished. He probably came to and climbed out of the window, no doubt. All that was left was to call the police officers. Those memories, though, those memories were haunting his waking moments, and tonight would haunt his dreams.

Hunter stood in the morgue, looking over at three slabs. All of them had white sheets over them, but that did little to hide the fact that there was a ton of bloodshed in this room. Hunter walked to the first slab and pulled the sheet to expose the face.

"Mr. Whitcomb, I presume," Hunter muttered as he took in the visuals. The man had put up a bit of a fight. There on his left cheek was a clear and fresh scratch mark. Hunter made a note of it and did his regular examination. Long story short, Hunter was confident that the cause of death was the gaping knife wound on the neck, but Hunter took no chances and decided to take blood. What was the harm in a bit of toxicology? Making his way to the following body, he pulled the sheet down. This one was Mrs. Whitcomb. Without the slash across her neck, she looked much more peaceful than her husband. His objective view was the same until he looked under her nails and found flesh. Did Mrs. Whitcomb attack her husband? Why? This brought up more questions than answers. Taking a sample, Hunter made his way to the last slab. This was the one that he was dreading. He couldn't stand to see small children in this state. It was bad enough from natural causes, but when someone went out of their way to harm a child, it made Hunter's blood boil. He couldn't imagine Hannah doing this to any of them, and some evidence backed up his theory.

Pulling back the sheet, the poor boy was in two pieces. How could Hannah do this? She wouldn't have the strength. The bones had been cut clean through, possibly using a bone saw. Where on Earth would she have gotten something like that? Then it hit him like a ton of bricks.

Entering the crime scene was a little more than Andrew had expected. There was blood and gore all over the house, so much so that the police forced him to put booties on his shoes before walking onto the grass and into the place. Officer Jenkins was waiting on the front porch for Drew, and his nose was shoved in his tiny notebook.

"What the hell happened here?" Andrew asked, adjusting his hat and looking around at all the hustle and bustle still going on around him.

"Hell, Drew, it's taking all day to process this crime scene. I don't know if it's part of your case, but it sure is a cluster fuck of a thing here." Andrew nodded, and they walked into the house. Andrew had

45

to use the sleeve of his coat to cover his nose. The smell of decay was almost too much to handle.

"We got your boy over at the morgue doing a preliminary exam on the bodies, but best we can figure Hannah went Plum nuts and butchered her family sometime early this morning. There was food cooking on the oven when we got her, and she was babbling some odd stuff."

"Babbling?" Andrew asked, "What exactly was she saying to you?"

"We have it on tape; I can try to get a copy to you, but you know it's got to be on the down-low; some of these other cops don't always think too highly of you, and I catch hell for helping. So, the less they know, the better." Andrew nodded as they continued on their walk through the house. Andrew could see the blood smeared down the hall. It had begun to look brown; if it weren't for the coolness of the season, he would have seen flies for sure.

"There was one thing I remember clearly; it was something she said repeatedly." Officer Jenkins began, "There was a man in her closet, but it was in her dream. At least she thought it was a man; it wore a mask. Also, something about a spell and her hand not healing."

"Does she have a wound on her hand?" Andrew asked.

"None that we could see." Andrew scratched his temple and thought for a moment.

"You think maybe she was drugged? Maybe she had some fever dream." Officer Jenkins shrugged his shoulder as they continued down the hall and into Hannah's bedroom. Everything was just as she had left it that morning. If Andrew hadn't seen all the blood in the kitchen, he would have thought that everything was the start of a typical weekend here at the Whitcomb house.

Drew quickly looked around the room and noticed that the bedroom window was left open.

"Has anyone dusted for prints over there at the window? That could be a point of entry." Jenkins nodded and looked back down at his little book.

"We gathered DNA evidence in the kitchen, took food samples just in case some hallucinogen was used, and took fingerprints from all points of entry, including the open window. We won't know anything for certain until your guy prints the bodies and sends the blood samples." When Jenkins finally looked at Andrew, he had made his way to Hannah's closet. Using a gloved hand, he opened the door and looked down at the ground.

The Whitcomb family had recently redecorated the house, including putting down fresh, white carpeting, the good kind. The kind that if someone were to stand in one place for too long, they would leave indents in the plush flooring. Andrew pointed down at the floor, and officer Jenkins walked over to see what the man had discovered.

"Were any of your men taking a coffee break in here?"

"No, why would you ask that?" Jenkins retorted as he looked down at what Drew was pointing at.

"It looks like someone was in here for quite some time, officer, and I highly doubt those footprints will match Hannah's." Before Andrew could say any more on the subject, his phone began to go off in his front pocket. Jenkins didn't know what was said, but it had to be crucial because Drew left in a hurry, which wasn't his usual course of action.

Will hadn't wanted to meet Claire, and he tried to put the whole thing behind him. He didn't want to see the woman that looked exactly like his dead girlfriend, but he was back in her apartment holding a mug of herbal tea like they were best friends.

It was a small town, and in small towns, word travels fast. Within hours the whole of Finch Hollow knew about the gruesome murders at the Whitcomb house. What they didn't know was what exactly happened and how many of them died. Claire couldn't take any chances. She had tried to call Matthew, but he didn't answer. On the other hand, William agreed to meet with her considering the situation.

"What do you mean?" Will asked as he put the tea on the counter. "Do you think me and Matt might be in some kind of danger?" Claire nodded and took another sip of her tea.

"I'm not sure exactly, but it's better to air on the side of caution in these types of... well, circumstances."

"What kind of circumstances would those be exactly?" Will didn't trust Claire, nope, not after what had happened a few nights back... Not when the hot searing pain in his hand was a constant reminder of what they had done and how it did nothing to save the love of his life.

"I'm sorry I didn't tell the three of you what was going on earlier; I didn't know how to explain, and to be honest, I didn't think you would have believed me. You have to understand we were so close to saving her, Will. We might still be able to if you can answer me one question."

"What is that exactly?" Will asked, grimacing. He couldn't bear the thought of never seeing Darla's face again.

"Do you still feel it? The heat from the spell? Is it still encompassing your hand?" William nodded, and he could see a smile cross Ms. Sneads face. It wasn't the smile of a loving mother; this was the smile of something sinister, and he didn't want anything more to do with it. William went to his feet and went to the front door but stopped halfway.

"You know something, Ms. Snead?" Clair got to her feet and made her way to the boy, still holding her drink.

"What is that, William?" She still had that smirk, sending a chill down the boy's spine.

"I'm going to go to church, and I'm going to pray for you. You used to be a sweet lady, and I know we are all grieving, but what you're doing... what we've been doing here is unnatural."

"It's unfortunate that you would say that, son,"

"And why is that?" Will asked but got his answer when Claire threw her drink in his face. Will wanted to cry out and yell at the old crone, but nothing came out. Falling face down on the dense wood floor, he could hear her cackle as everything around him faded to black.

"Why couldn't you drink your tea like a good boy instead? It will take a lot of polish to fix the damage to my floor, which is antique wood!" Grabbing William by the wrists, Claire dragged him down the hall and into the spare bedroom. Claire managed to get him onto the bed with all her strength. "There you go, William; I hope you're comfy. Cause that's where you're staying until this is all over, and I have no use for you. The body can go without food and water for at least three days, sometimes longer if you don't exert yourself, and I don't think you'll be doing much of anything for a while." Clair let out another cackle as she shut the bedroom door behind her. Nothing was going to stop her from getting her daughter back, no, nothing, including killing. There was a lot more going on here than meets the eye, and only one person could help her finish her goal; his name was Andrew Bower.

Hunter had just finished the preliminary exam of the Whitcomb family when Andrew walked through the morgue doors. He had yet to scrub up, which could only mean one thing: Hunter would be left alone in the basement to finish this gory story himself.

"What was so urgent that you had to pull me away from the new crime scene? I'm sure there was more that I had yet to discover." Several hours had passed, and it was well past midnight; Hunter picked up his metal file and flipped through the pages for a second.

"There might be more here than at the scene this time, Drew," Hunter muttered. Taking his eyes away from the file and putting them on his friend. "It would seem that there was quite a struggle from Mr.

Whitcomb, but none of the other bodies had signs of a struggle. Answer me this, Drew, if Hannah were the killer, wouldn't she have defensive wounds on her somewhere? I spoke to the intake officer tonight, and even though she was talking nonsense, she didn't have a scratch on her." Again, Andrew scratched his head, which he always tended to do when deep in thought.

"I didn't think she was our guy anyway. She's a little slip of a thing, and honestly, I couldn't imagine her taking down her parents single-handedly."

"And then there's this," Hunter said as he made his way to the Whitcomb boy and removed the sheet. "How in the world would a teenage girl get the strength to sever a human head with a butcher knife? The cut was clean, and the bones weren't splintered. I have my suspicions that if she were involved in her family's death, she wouldn't act alone. There's only one tool I can think of that would cut this precisely, and you know what that is."

"A bone saw," Drew interjected, and Hunter nodded in agreement.

"It got me thinking about whom might have access to something like that; I mean, you can't just walk into a medical supply store and order one, and then you would have to know exactly how to use it."

"What exactly are you getting at Hunter?" Throwing the sheet back over the boy's body, Hunter walked over to Drew, placing the file on the desk beside him.

"What I'm getting at is Friday night, I ran into Kelly."

"What is so odd about that?" Drew asked. "She works here; she's a nurse, so that we will see her from time to time."

"Yes," Hunter agreed, "But not in the basement and not as late in the evening as it was. It didn't occur to me then that it was odd, but once I saw the boy's wounds, it raised my eyebrow."

"I could understand why," Andrew added as he walked out the door. "I will add it to my list of things to look into. Tomorrow I have a prior engagement."

"Oh?" Hunter questioned, "With who?"

"A rather well-versed town historian. I have a four-hundred-year-old mystery to solve."

Darla had been watching television for what felt like forever, and she had begun to grow restless. Pacing the floor between the couch and the kitchen, she could feel the cabin fever begin to close in on her. It wasn't that bad when the guys were here; at least she had company, but the two of them had left her alone in the house without a return phone number to call. What if they had forgotten about her? What if they never come back? Fear and panic begin to set in, and all logic left the building. She didn't know what to do or where to go, but she knew she couldn't stay there. Something terrible was coming, and she could feel it building up inside her chest like a silent scream that she couldn't let out.

Opening the closet door in the back bedroom, Darla snatched one of Hunter's hoodies and slipped out the back, leaving the television on with only a half-eaten turkey sandwich as its audience.

Darla knew she had cleaned out Hunter's kitchen and probably eaten her body weight in food, but her stomach had begun to growl again, and the insatiable hunger that she had felt a few hours before had returned three-fold. What was it that she needed? She hadn't a clue. The crisp fall breeze nipped at her face as she went down the road, but she paid it no mind. All she could think about now was food.

Within thirty minutes, Darla was standing at the base of the old church, just a few hundred feet from where her lifeless body had laid, and her new life had merely begun. She had to find out what happened, and soon, she hated hiding from her mother and friends; she hated that people thought she had died... Or had she? Her memories had begun to get a little foggy, and the vision in her right eye was fading in and out. She had neglected to tell Hunter about it because she didn't want either of the men to stop their search for the truth and the killer. She knew as well as everyone else in town that those kids didn't kill themselves. Everyone just enjoyed sticking their heads in the sand and pretending that nothing was even the littlest bit odd in Finch Hollow; hell, how could a place so close to Coral Bay not have its weirdness? Darla had heard the stories as a child, and her mother had even professed that she had once lived on the south side, which was not the best of places.

Darla turned to return to the house when she bumped into someone in passing. Instinctively she looked up, coming face to face with Father Hall. At first, the man looked confused, but then a sly smile washed across his lips.

"A little early for Sunday mass, aren't we, child." Brushing past the man, Darla began to quicken her gait, wrapping her arms around herself as a sudden chill coursed through her body. It wasn't from the cold, though; no, it was from Father Hall's icy gaze boring a hole through her soul.

When Darla had made her way back to the house, Andrew had parked himself on the couch beside the turkey sandwich.

"Where have you been?" He asked in a deep voice.

"I... I." Darla couldn't finish her thought. Everything had begun to get swimmy. Her vision was fading, and a sudden heat wave flashed across her flesh. Pulling the hoodie off, she could feel the cotton tear at the hole in the side of her head. Growling in pain, she fell to her knees. Andrew could hear the struggle in her voice and got to his feet when he heard her fall.

"Darla, are you okay?" He asked as he knelt beside her, putting a gingered hand across her back. Darla looked up at the man; he could see the pleading in her eyes, and he could also see that she was not improving. Her right eye was a milky shade of white now, indicating a cataract, and the wound on her head had begun to smell. It was a smell that the man knew all too well, and it was the smell of decomposition.

"Let's get you to bed," Andrew said as he helped the young woman.

"What's happening to me?" Darla whispered.

"We are still unsure, but we are doing our best to find out." Andrew laid the girl on the bed and quickly shut the door. She didn't have much time, for that he was sure. He just hoped that Mark Randolph had more answers for him.

Matt had spent the night in the ICU with his father. It had taken quite a bit of convincing by a pretty nurse to make him go home and get some rest. The police had gone and written it off as some botched robbery. Case closed, right?

Matt knew there was more to it than that and decided without delay to stop at nothing to end whoever hurt his father. Pushing the button on the answering machine, he had a slew of added information thrown at him from all directions. The first was from Claire Snead.

"Hello, Matthew, I'm sure you've heard about what happened to Hannah and her family early this morning, and I was hoping to speak with you and William regarding this matter. You have my direct line. I look forward to hearing from you." There was a click on the other end of the line, and the voicemail went to the following message.

"Hello, this message is for Davis Winters. I'm officer Henry Jenkins, trying to put a few pieces together regarding the Whitcomb family. Without giving away too much over the phone, we are just reaching out, hoping to talk to you and your son Matthew. If you could call us back at the Finch Hollow police station at your earliest convenience, that would be great. Thank you." Again, the line clicked off, and Matt stood in the kitchen with a look of confusion on his face. What had happened the night of his attack? Did Hannah get hurt? There were too many questions in his head to count, but he knew that if his friends were being attacked, Claire had something to do with it, and that is where he would start.

Andrew had forced himself to sleep and found himself on the road with Darla in the back seat. After last night's debacle, he felt it frugal to keep an eye on her twenty-four-seven. Hunter hadn't returned from the morgue, which meant one of two things. Either he is hot on the trail of another lead or fell asleep in his desk chair again. Andrew had to give it to the kid; he was ruthless when searching for the truth, and Drew was proud to have someone like that on his side.

"Where are we going again?" Darla asked, slurring her words a little. Darla reminded Andrew of a drunk toddler, which pained him. Merely last Friday, she talked and acted quite like an average teenager.

"I told you before, and we are going to see Mark Randolph from Eagles Nest. He is supposed to be the best historian around here, and I need to know why all of this is happening." Darla silently nodded and slid down in her seat. Sleep did not favor the girl; if anything, her situation had worsened once the sun had risen. If he were to get pulled over, there would be a lot of explaining to do.

Zelda wasn't lying when she told him it was a bit of a drive, but when he pulled up to the three-story cabin, he knew he had arrived at the correct place.

"Big house." Darla mused as Andrew turned the engine off, and they both got out of the car. Walking up to the front door Drew reached up to ring the doorbell, but the door swung open, and a more petite, plump man with a balding head smiled a big smile and held out a hand. Andrew shook it, and the three of them walked inside the cabin. Making their way through the front hallway and into the conservatory, Mr. Randolph motioned for them to sit at a large wooden table facing a rather tall bookshelf. Andrew couldn't help but wonder how the little man could reach the top shelf.

After the three of them were seated, the man pulled an old leather-bound book from the bookshelf behind them.

"Well, Mr. Bower, what exactly did you want to know about the history of Finch Hollow? What was it? In the..." The man opened the book and looked through it for a second. He had to pick up and put on a wire-framed pair of reading glasses to ensure he had correctly found what he was looking for. "Ah, yes, the 1600's." When Mark looked up, it was almost like he had seen Darla for the first time. "Why hello, their young lady. My name is Mark Randolph." Reaching out a hand, Mark waited for the girl to shake it, but instead, she leaned over the table and began to smell his hand. The man pulled back his hand, a little confused.

"You will have to excuse Da... I mean Tammy. She had recent; brain trauma; we hope she will have a complete recovery." Mark opened his mouth to say something regarding Tammy's condition but thought better of it and waited for Andrew to tell him exactly why he had come.

"Well, I'm not sure if this has any relevance to the case I'm working on, but I have an acquaintance that told me about this colony that settled here in the 1600s Maynor's wisp?" Mark's eyes lit up like lights at the sound of the colony's name.

"Oh! You want information on the death curse."

"Death curse?" Drew asked as he took his hat off and scooted closer to the man with extreme interest.

"Well, for lack of a better word. You know, Mr. Bower, some of this information cannot be proven one way or the other. I hope you weren't counting on fact-checking this in any way because I took a major interest in this when I wrote my doctorate. It's tranquil, a delightful read, though." While the two men were talking, Darla began to look around the room. A tiny bit of drool began to fall from her mouth. It was a good thing that Mark was so into his book, or the possibility of him noticing would have been relatively good.

"Okay, so the original five families of Maynor's Wisp were founded in 1625. The one family in the forefront was pastor Archer Wilson and his wife, Rebecca."

"Wait, what were the last names of the other four families?" Drew asked as he pulled a notebook from his front pocket.

"Let's take a look here." Estimating the book in front of him, Mark pointed at something on the page. "Here we go. It looks like there were the Wilsons, the Connors, the Wallers, the Lancasters, and the Sneads."

"Is that so..." Drew began.

'Does that mean anything to you?" Mark asked

"Yes. This might not have been a waste of time after all."

"Well, learning about the town's history is never a waste of time, but I can see where you're going with that statement, so no offense taken. Right across the river was the town you know as Finch Hollow. They had only been there a year before this new little group came along, and they both took up fishing as their primary export. It didn't take too long before the two colonies crossed paths. Sometimes it was at the farmers' markets across the lands, and because the two groups came from different regions, they both had different sets of diseases. Well, that's what the original story would like you to believe."

"What does that mean?" Andrew asked. The two of them were so obsessed with the information on the table that neither noticed when Darla got up from the table. They didn't hear the sound of the open front door and certainly didn't notice that she had taken a particular book on the end table by the conservatory exit.

"Well, many strange and unusual things tended to happen at Maynor's wisp. Sometimes travelers would be invited to stay with them, and then they would disappear into the night. Because there were no bodies to prove that something strange was happening, the founding colony had no way of getting rid of them. In my humble opinion, the pastor of Fishers Bay, or Finch Hollow as we call it now, hatched a plan to eliminate Maynor's Wisp. It did not go well."

"How so?" Andrew asked as he slid ever closer to Mr. Randolph.

"Well, the Hall family had strong ties to the church, and it was said that the oldest son Robert snuck across the river in the dead of night to poison the day's catch. So, when they went to market the next day, the colony of Maynor's Wisp would make everyone sick, and the people would stop buying from them. Needless to say, the boy was caught and became another statistic. They were gone by the sun's first light. Of course, the Wilson family swore that the boy ran off with their oldest daughter Rose, and she was never heard from again. It still seems hard to believe to me. There was a turf war; as you can see, no one had died of mysterious illness... yet."

"So, it's coming, right?" Mark smiled at the man and nodded his head.

"So, after the botched attempt at sabotage, the people of Fischer's Bay began to drop like flies, leaving all but the pastor and two of his trusted parish members too sick to do anything, and with the colder weather coming, they had nothing left to do but call a truce. So the man crossed the river to confront the five families. After that, things get a bit foggy, to be honest."

"What does that mean?" Drew asked. His attention was still on the man and not directed towards the girl who had wandered into the wilderness and unfamiliar territory.

"Well, as I said before, Andrew, some of this was put in by people who merely guessed what happened. I've tried to prove and disprove scenarios but with no luck. Maybe you will have a better chance than I did of figuring it all out."

"I certainly hope so, my friend. Other lives might be at stake."

"So, the pastor never returned, and the two perish members were left to starve in a town full of sick and dying people. On the last night, it was said they struck a deal with a wandering traveler. It was the last night that Fischer's Bay technically existed. That's when the death curse was turned towards the five families of Maynor's wisp. Of course, I don't have it, and even if I did, I wouldn't give it to you or read it out loud. I don't know if you're a spiritual type of fellow, but I have no intention of conjuring up any bad mojo. From what I gathered, though. Each family would endure hardships, and on the cusp of the fifth generation, the last of those bloodlines would perish, thus breaking the curse and awakening something else."

"Did anyone tell us what that something else might be?" Andrew asked, and Mark shook his head.

"Nope, but in my experience, it's nothing good like a box of puppies." Mark let out a snorted laugh and finally looked around the room. "Hey, didn't you have a little girl with you?" Andrew got to his feet with a start.

"Oh shit. Darl... I mean Tammy!" Drew began to holler as he made his way to the front door. He knew immediately that the girl had wandered off and down the mountain. Mark followed closely behind Andrew.

"Would you like me to call the police?" Mark asked.

"No, that won't be needed," Drew muttered.

"Why would that be?" Mark retorted.

"Because I work with the police," Andrew stated as he pulled the keys from his pant pocket. I will find her on the way down the mountain, and I will undoubtedly call Eagle's Nest PD if I don't." Mark silently nodded and let the man get in his yellow hooptie and squeal down the road. Little did the man know that someone was waiting for him... Someone that would be coming under the blanket of night, and this person did not have his best interests at heart.

Andrew drove down the driveway while he fumbled in the seat beside him, looking for his cell phone. There was only one person he wanted to talk to now: Hunter. He hadn't spent this time away from him when they were on an active case, and he needed to tell Hunter about the emergence and what he had found out at Mark Randolph's house. With any luck, he will spot Darla on the way down the hill, but her condition worried Andrew more and more each minute. Andrew finally found his phone and pushed the speed dial.

"Hello?" Hunter answered on the second ring. He usually did when he was at home.

"Hunter, we have a situation." Drew began but was cut off by Hunter, who seemed more than excited to tell Drew about something that couldn't wait.

"Yes, we do!" Drew could hear his friend pacing the hallway, more than likely chewing on his thumbnail; it was a nervous habit the boy had, and in all five years that Drew had known him, it had only worsened. "You will never believe what happened on the same night as the Whitcomb triple homicide."

"What?" Drew asked as he kept a keen eye out for Darla or even a hint of where she might have gone. Drew didn't think the girl had a lot of who about her anymore, which would make her a lot harder to find than if she had an agenda.

"So," Hunter stated, "There was a break-in on the other side of town at the same time as, well, you know. The thing is that the two kids know each other and get this... Someone cut a hole in this other kid's left hand,"

"You mean like the hand that Hannah kept complaining hurt so much? Are you suggesting they have some telepathy?" Andrew could hear Hunter scoff under his breath and then try to compose himself as he continued with his story.

"I highly doubt that is the case because the girl was talking about something that happened a few days before. What I'm getting at is this kid might know a little more than he's letting on. You want to know who this kid is, Drew?"

"Of course," Andrew retorted as he took a hard right on the one-lane dirt road.

Matthew Dunbar, Davis Dunbar's only son."

"And the Godson to a one Chairperson Howards. Oh, I am sure he's livid. Did he call you?"

"Yes, he said he tried to call you first, but I know how you are." Andrew pulled the phone away from his head and realized he had three missed calls.

"Why do I always do this to myself?" Drew muttered.

"What?" Hunter asked.

"Nothing," Drew could feel a tension headache beginning to brew in his temples. If he didn't have to babysit Darla, he could be back on his way into town to talk to Matt and his father, but he couldn't in good conscience leave the poor girl to the elements. She would be eaten alive by coyotes. She did, after all, reek of death. "Tell Chairperson Howards I will be there first thing in the morning to talk to the two of them myself."

"No can do, buddy," Hunter began

"And why is that?" Drew asked as he took a deep breath, popping his jaw.

"You can probably talk to Matt, but his dad took a pretty bad stab wound to the gut, and they have him in the ICU for the foreseeable future. No visitors apart from immediate family."

"You should know one thing about me by now, Hunter, and there is always a way around things. That is if you try. Oh, and I lost Darla."

"YOU WHAT??" Hunter yelled. Drew almost dropped the phone onto the floorboard but managed to hold it, even if he almost hit a tree.

"Yeah, she slipped out the door when Mark and I were talking. There's one more thing, Hunter, she doesn't look the way you remember. She looks more like...."

"You're standard run-of-the-mill dead girl walking?" Hunter mused.

"For lack of a better term... I don't know what happened. She was fine, and then she just started to... fall apart."

"I knew something wasn't right as soon as she started to eat everything in the house," Hunter said. Drew could hear the Refrigerator door open and close. "She even ate the raw chicken in the crisper. Does that sound fine to you? We have to figure out what happened."

"I agree, Hunter, but first, I have to find her."

Matt didn't waste much time calling Claire back and rushing to her apartment. The exact old-fashioned bellboy stood at the front of the door, not saying a single word. For some reason, the man always creeped Matt out. There was something... off about him. But that wasn't the reason for today's visit. Today's visit was about what had happened the night before and why anyone would have wanted to hurt him or his father. Matt knew his father didn't have any enemies, and after his mother left, he didn't even have the heart to remarry, let alone date anyone. They both lived solitary lives and tended to like it that way.

Making his way up the steps, he could see Claire waiting for him, leaning over the railing with a look of concern on her face. Matt knew that was her go-to look when trying to convince someone something was entirely wrong in her happy bubble. Motioning him to enter the apartment, she vanished into the open door, and Matt followed a few moments later.

When he walked inside, he saw Ms. Snead sitting in her chair on the far side of the room. Two cups of warm tea welcomed him, and he silently shut the door behind him: making his way to the couch adjacent to her.

"I don't want to hear some rantings of a grieving mother right now, Ms. Snead." Matt began, "I need to know why someone would attack my father and me last night and try to kill us." Claire picked up the mug of tea in front of her and motioned to Matt's hand with her eyes.

"They do that to you?" Matt nodded. "Well, after what happened to Hannah and you, I do not doubt that my suspicions are validated."

"What might those be?" Matt said; the scowl on his face was more than Claire needed to know beyond a doubt that she had to choose her words carefully.

"You know what happened to Hannah, don't you, Matt?" Matthew shook his head no and picked the mug up from the table. The warm liquid inside the cup comforted the throbbing wound on his left hand. "The cops think she did it, but I tell you, I have my doubts. Someone came into their house in the dead of night, at the same time as you were being assaulted, I would measure to guess, and killed her whole family." Matt's eyes widened with horror and shock. He had been to her house on more than one occasion, sat at the dinner table, and spent time with her brother.

"Even little Chris?" Claire nodded.

"Yes, even little Chris. When the police showed up, she was in the corner, mumbling about some intruder. That's all I know, and I know that much because I have friends on the town board. We have to stick together, us three now."

"But why Ms. Snead? Why would someone want to hurt us?" Matt couldn't help but take a sip of his tea. The smell was intoxicating. With a smile, the woman sat her mug back on the table.

"I'm going to be straight with you, Matthew. I feel, at this point, I owe you that much. There are two sides to this story, and you don't want to be caught on the wrong side; I can assure you of that." Matt could feel the tips of his fingers and toes begin to tingle, and he let the tea slip from his fingers. "Some might call me evil, hell, I've been called a lot worse in my time, but the one thing I will not have is my daughter's soul sacrificed just because some of my lineages didn't practice great choices in their day." Claire laughed and threw up her hands as she got to her feet and walked over to the boy, who could barely keep his head up. "I'm not one for giving away everything in some torrid verbal vomit of a confession, but I will tell you this, if she goes, the curse will be lifted, and

75

something far worse is going to reign down on all of our heads. Something no one is prepared to take on, not even Andrew Bower... Whom I'm positive will visit me once you and your little friend William come up missing." Claire's smile widened as she motioned at the closed door over her shoulder. "Yeah, he beat you here." Matt tried to open his mouth, but nothing would come out; it took all he could do without blinking, and the room began to fade out as he fell into unconsciousness.

Hunter walked up to the front door of 1515 Spring Front Lane. He knew where Kelly lived all too well. When he had first moved into town, he had taken her out on a few dates, but they never really ended up in a relationship; however, they have remained friends ever sense. He could see an unknown beat-up white pick-up truck parked on the curb and couldn't help but wonder who it was.

Over the last few years, the two of them had not been as close over the previous few years, but Hunter was sure that if she had started dating someone, she would have for sure told him about it. It would have been a fabulous water cooler convo, and if she hadn't told him, she would have for sure told the other nurses, who would have eventually told him. The hospital was good for the gossip.

Knocking on the front door, Hunter could hear rustling and then heated whispers. He couldn't determine what was being said on the other side of the door, but they couldn't seem to agree on whatever it was. Leaning his head against the wooden front door glass, he thought he could hear Kelly say something to the effects of 'Leave him alone.' And then 'Big trouble.' Standing up at attention and backing away from the door, he could hear footsteps coming closer and someone turning the handle.

Kelly and Hunter stood face to face at the front door, and the man could tell something wasn't right. Kelly fidgeted from foot to foot, and she wrang her hands in front of her like she was washing them.

"Is everything okay, Kelly?"

"Yeah... Yes, everything is alright. Why wouldn't it be? It's my day off, and you know that." Hunter smiled and nodded. Pointing at the truck behind him, he tilted his head in a questioning manner.

"That yours?" Hunter asked as he tried to look past her into the little house, but Kelly was doing her best not to let him. Hunter thought he could see movement in the room behind her, but he couldn't be sure.

"Look, what are you doing here, Hunter? I have plans later and need to get ready." He knew this was her way of changing the subject, but he allowed her to do so.

"Well, see, here's the thing, Kelly, last Friday, I saw you in the basement, and it was real late for you to be at work."

"I was picking up extra shifts. I'm trying to... Make payments on that truck, you see, and um, I'm sick of carpooling with Kevin. He never lets me pick the music... And I think his little battery-operated, wind-up car is pretentious." Hunter knew that she was lying. Her nervousness only worsened, and she couldn't even look him in the eye.

"Alrighty... well then you will see my interest in your whereabouts that the following night, unfortunately, the Whitcomb family was killed, and at first glance, we all thought maybe the girl had gone little nuts. What with the ranting and hallucinations and all?" Hunter was cut off again by Kelly, whose voice had magnified and become more manic.

"That's right! I heard that it was an open and cut case. That Hannah girl, she's nuttier than a pecan pie. Yeah, that's what I heard, all right." Kelly let her guard down long enough for Hunter to see clear past her and into the room she had been trying to keep him from seeing. Sure enough, there was a man, probably in his mid to late twenties. He had short black hair and wore blue jeans and a white beater. He had a beer in one hand and listened intently to the conversation.

"You see, here's the thing." Hunter began as he put a finger up for Kelly to listen. The woman grew silent and finally looked up at the man. She was afraid of what was going to come out of his mouth. She thought she had been careful enough and covered her tracks, but she knew Hunter and Andrew were good at what they did.

"Once I had the chance to look at the boy's body, I knew that decapitation of this precise manner couldn't have been done with a butcher knife; I mean, you would have to have super strength to pull that off, and Hannah, I mean have you seen how small she is?? I doubt she could open a pickle jar."

"What are you getting at Hunter? Like I said...."

"Yeah yeah, I heard you the first time. Kelly, I know you stole a bone saw from the morgue. We have motion sensor cameras in there for that exact reason. I also know you tried to hide your face from them, but you couldn't hide that red hair. The only question I have, you know, before I turn you and your little buddy into the police, is this... Why?" Only now did the man finally get to his feet and say a word.

"Why don't you come in, Hunter? We can explain everything. It's not what you think." Kelly lifted her hand in protest, but Hunter pushed past her, and she followed, shutting the door behind her. They all made their way into the living room, and the man in the white beater plopped down on the couch with his beer still in hand. Lifting it toward Hunter, he smiled, the most friendly smile he had ever seen; to Hunter, this man looked like he didn't have a care in the world.

"It would seem as if I have you at a disadvantage. I know your name, but you don't know me, and I find that very rude of Kelly not to introduce us. My name is Connor, Connor Biggs. You might say I work with Ms. Kelly on a more... personal level."

"Is that your way of saying you two are dating?" Connor let out a laugh that echoed through the house. It was a loud and unsettling sound for Hunter, and he could tell that Kelly didn't like it much either.

"I guess since you caught us with our pants down, we should go ahead and tell you the whole thing. You must know, though, that there are more of us, like a LOT more of us, and you may want to reconsider the notion of turning us in. I'm just saying you can cut off the head, but two more will grow back, and I mean, the devil you know is probably better than the one you don't." Hunter refused to sit down; he had kept his eyes directly on the two killers and didn't want them to get the upper hand. Kelly had sat on the other side of the couch and, yet again, refused to make direct eye contact with either of them.

"Well, go ahead there, Connor, spit it out; what lame reason did you two have for killing a perfectly innocent family."

"I wouldn't say all that; I would call it... convenient. You see, our reason for doing what we did was one of the best reasons I could think of. Power. If you do everything exactly right when this dinky curse thing is broken, the real big bad will bring you power. I've spent my whole life crawling my way out of shitholes like this, working at shit jobs with shit people and never getting anywhere. I'm ready for it to be my turn, you understand?"

"Not really." Hunter began. Connor took the last sip of his beer and put it on the table before him.

"You want a beer?" He asked, and Hunter shook his head no, "Well, I'm getting another beer." Connor got to his feet and vanished into the kitchen.

"Can you shed some light on what he's saying?" Hunter asked as he leaned against the door frame.

"You're not going to believe me; I'm sure Andrew has more information on the curse than I do. I guess those two parts were left separated because knowledge is power. Once the bloodline is severed, the Beast will arise, and a new darkness will cover the land."

"So, you want the apocalypse?" Hunter asked, scratching his head.

"No, it's a reign of power, and all those who side with the Beast will be rewarded great power and strength. First, a blood sacrifice must be made to destroy the offending families. A man, a woman, and a virgin child. We thought killing the Whitcomb's and framing Hannah would kill two birds with one stone."

"How so?" Hunter asked. He was so interested in what Kelly said that he didn't see Connor slip back in the front door with a shovel in hand. He didn't notice Kelly's eyes darting around like a caged animal. All Hunter was focused on was answers; the ones he was getting were vague.

"Because we need to cut off the girl's hand!" Connor yelled as he swung the shovel at Hunter's head. Hunter ducked at the right time and hit Connor in the stomach with a solid left hook. Kelly jumped up and let out a little shriek as she began to inch her way to the back door.

The two men rolled around on the floor, hitting the table in front of the couch, knocking magazines, remotes, and one glass beer bottle onto the carpeted floor beside them. Connor had his hands around Hunter's throat, but that didn't stop the man from punching his assailant right in the face with a solid right jab; he could hear the snap of Connor's nose, and blood began to spray all over Hunter's shirt and Connor's white beater turning it a dark shade of red.

"My nose!" Connor yelled as he let go of Hunter's throat and put it over his face. Grabbing the beer bottle, Hunter smashed it against the table. Shards of glass flew everywhere, but what was left in his hands made a great knife. Try as he might to push the man off him, Connor was unmoved; in fact, Hunter was pretty sure he could physically feel the rage bubble up into the man's chest. Letting out a battle cry, Conner began to wale on Hunter with wide, fury-infused punches that contacted his face, chest, and throat. Hunter could feel himself waver, and he was almost at the point of unconsciousness. He had only one option. Taking the broken beer bottle, Hunter thrust the sharp glass into Connor's side, causing him to fall off of Hunter and roll onto his belly.

"You stabbed me, you fucker!" Connor yelled in a heated rage. Getting to his feet, Hunter grabbed the shovel from the doorway and hit him with the blunt end, knocking Connor out like a light. Looking around the room, he knew in an instant that Kelly had made her great escape, but that didn't stop Hunter from calling the police and telling them everything that had happened at 1515 Spring Front Lane.

The sun was setting behind the massive cabin on the hill by Eagles Nest. Mark had sat by the large bay window on the first floor. He had a rather large cup of hot chocolate in his hand. He had been watching the first snowfall of the year start up around an hour after Andrew had left his house. Now that the sun had begun to set, he could still make out the lights from the investigator's car rolling back down the hill in a desperate attempt at finding Darla. Yes, Mark knew exactly who the girl was when he had first laid eyes on her. She was a little worse for wear since the first time he had seen her, but her features were undeniable even under the worst circumstances. He felt he knew why the girl was the way she was, and to be honest, he thought, at least for the time being, who was responsible.

The doorbell rang, and Mark looked down at his watch.

"Seven thirty? Who could be here at this hour and in this weather?" He asked himself as he put the hot cup of cocoa on the window seal and walked to his front door.

On the other side was a familiar face accompanied by two he had not seen before. The one in the far back had a rather large head wound and didn't look like he enjoyed being here at this hour in this weather any more than Mark liked the company.

"Zelda, what on earth are you doing here?" Mark hissed as the woman pushed herself inside, and the other two followed.

"You know exactly why we are here, Mr. Randolph. We agreed you would tell Mr. Bowers what we spoke about and nothing more."

"And that's what I did," Mark said but was cut off by the man with the head wound.

"Why are you helping these people? Can't you see you have to let this play out the way it was meant to? They are an abomination." Zelda held a hand up, and the man quickly shut his mouth.

"Ethan, what did we say bout talking out of turn." Zelda barked. The man looked down at his feet and got back in line.

"I'm sorry, ma'am, it won't happen again."

"I did exactly what you told me to do, Zelda." Mark began to sputter.

"Well, yes and no. Who's idea was it to shroud the girl? Let her escape, and with the book, no less!! She's a drooling idiot, and god knows where she is at this point."

"You forgot something about that drooling idiot Zelda," Mark said as he returned to the window that held his sugary comfort.

"What's that, Mr. Randolph," Zelda said as she moved closer to the man. She had nothing but contempt in her eyes for the old schlub.

"If you've done what I think you have, she is now quite dangerous as well." Mark took a sip of his hot cocoa and gaged the room. The two men looked at each other in quiet concern, but Zelda smirked.

"What is it that you think I've done to the child? The last time I checked, I couldn't even access her. If I had that ability, she would think of going through a woodchipper by now." Mark Gazed out the window. He could still see Andrew's headlights, but they were heading back up the mountain this time.

"The mother gave energy spirals to three of Darla's friends. She has the fourth; Darla should have completely healed by now, but she looks like an extra in a zombie film, so here is what I assume you did. You removed one of the energy spirals, and now she's not firing on all cylinders. Am I warm?" Zelda turned her nose up at the man.

"So, that doesn't make her dangerous, just stinky." Zelda hissed, and Mark scoffed as the two men continued to listen in confusion and fear.

"The body has this remarkable way of trying to self-preserve. Once Darla hits the wall, she will fight to regain that energy and self-heal. She will crave human flesh."

"Like a zombie?" Ethan asked. He couldn't keep his mouth shut any longer. Mark could see the fear in his eyes and knew he had caught at least one of them in the headlights.

"Not exactly; you see, it's not an infection, she won't turn you, but she would most likely kill you and any other living morsel that had whatever it was she would need.

"Now you see, guys, this is exactly what THEY want you to think; it's all part of the preservation plan. We take her energy, and she dies. It's as simple as that. The only reason that little rotting corpse had enough thought in her brain to take the book is that her little witch mommy somehow has a psychic link to her. Don't let this little troll get into your head."

Zelda motioned for the two to take the man, and they did as they were told. Ethan on the left and the other man on the right drug him by his arms out of the study and into the front yard. Mr. Randolph's hot cocoa fell to the ground, the mug and contents shattering and leaving a puddle on the solid wood floor.

Once they were outside, Mark looked up at the woman. The two men had pushed him to his knee. It had become blisteringly cold, and the sun had set entirely. They would have been in complete darkness except that the motion light in the driveway had kicked on when they all stepped outside.

"What are you doing, Zelda? Do you want a full-blown war, or are you just stupid?" Pulling the gun from her purse, she pointed it at the man's head.

"I'm not afraid of a few old dusty scholars coming after me because their buddy got offed. We are many, and you are few."

"That may be true, but we have one thing you don't."

"And what might that be?" Zelda hissed.

"Andrew Bower!" The voice came out of the shadows, but the woman knew exactly who it was.

"Andrew!" Zelda yelled from behind her. "If you know what's good for you, you will get in your squealy car right now and go home. This doesn't concern you!" There was a long pause, and Zelda's attention became squarely on Mark again. "Now where were...." But the woman was cut off by a colossal snowball hitting her in the back of the head. It took her by surprise, so much so that she pulled the trigger on the handgun and grazed Ethan in the shoulder.

"AHH," Ethan yelled and let go of Mark, who tried like hell to get to his feet, but the man had a firm grip. "What the hell, Zelda!!" Blood began to trickle from the open wound, and blood patterns started forming in the pure white snow.

"Looks like you're a crack shot there, Zelda. No wonder they let you have the gun." Yelling rage, the woman vanished around the side of the house, leaving Ethan to sit in the snow and sulk about another wound.

"First this head wound, Kevin, and now I get shot! By Zelda, no less. If it weren't for bad luck...." Ethan grew quiet when he saw the look on Kevin's face. "She's right behind me, isn't she?" Kevin nodded as he let go of Mark and began to run to the jeep they had come up in. Mark made it to the front door before he heard Ethen's screams.

Darla was hungry, not in the traditional sense of the word, but she was starving, and the smell of fresh blood brought her out of hiding. Ethan could barely get to his feet from the blood loss, which gave Darla the advantage.

"No, no, we can help you. You don't have to do this." Ethan stammered as she advanced on him, sinking her rotten teeth into his fresh wound. Screaming in fear and pain, the man began to flail and kick as he fell to the ground, but it was to no avail. She had gotten the better of him, and shock had already begun to flow through Ethan's cooling body.

"Where are you, you little maggot!" Zelda barked as she blindly wandered into the backside of the house.

"Everywhere and nowhere." She could hear Andrew's voice, it almost sounded as if he were above her, but it was so dark she couldn't see a thing. Zelda began to retreat to the jeep once the waning sound of screams echoed through the front of the house.

"We will have our time, you and I, Drew. You can bank on it." Zelda ran to the front of the house, and the two drove away in a heated escape. Darla had managed to hide well enough that Zelda hadn't seen, but there was no denying the carnage on the front lawn.

Andrew had climbed through a first-story window before Zelda had made her way to the backyard. He wasn't sure what happened out there, but there was no denying the screams. Now the two men were standing in front of each other, and Andrew had questions before he left for the night.

"What the hell was that?" Andrew asked, his voice was a little heated, but he tried to maintain his composure; he knew that he would get more answers by being civil than by flying off the handle.

"Look, I'm not going to sugarcoat anything here, seeing as I feel I was doing the right thing and saying the things I did today. Did I leave out some things? Sure, but I thought that would buy me some time."

"Buy you time? What exactly does that mean?" Andrew scanned the room; nothing seemed out of place, and there was no sign of Darla anywhere.

"Look, there seems to be some kind of confusion about whose side I'm on."

"And whose side would that be?" Andrew asked as he leaned against the wall, crossing his arms over his chest. He knew things weren't always as they seemed, but it looked confident that Zelda had baited him and possibly Claire. There were things that those women were hiding, and he could bet the farm that they were at the root of some of the not-so-cordial stuff that had been going on around town.

"I'm on my side Mr. Bower, and Zelda cannot wrap her head around it. You see, she and I, our families, at least originated from Fischer's Bay and were the founding members of what you might call a cult. Well, for all intent and purpose, it's THE cult you've been looking into, even if you didn't realize it until now. They tend to keep a low profile unless they have to." Mr. Randolph took a deep breath, walked over to the wooden chair that complemented the end table on the far side of the room, and took a seat. "You must forgive me, Andrew; it's been quite a rousing evening. I don't believe I've ever been that close to death before. I do owe you a great debt for saving me. I doubt I was not the first person you've saved over the years." Andrew nodded,

"It was nothing; I didn't think Zelda was that trigger-happy, shooting one of her men. Oh well, I guess it comes with the job, I suppose." Mark let out a little snort.

"Yeah, I wouldn't worry too much about that guy. What's left of him is on my front lawn." Andrew's brow furrowed, and he walked toward the man with concern.

"What did I miss?" Drew asked; Mark leaned forward and rubbed his temples with a heavy hand.

"Well, for starters, I wished you would have come to me before Darla got in that kind of condition; now we are going to have to lock her down until we can put an end to this... One way or the other." Andrew gave the man another confused look, and again, Mark sighed and continued. "The cult of idiots takes blind orders from someone in the church; to say for certain would be anyone's guess. Most think it's Father Hall, but I honestly don't know. That's above my pay grade. Someone gave the green light to do something stupid."

"What would that be, Mr. Randolph, I don't have all night, and I'm sure Darla is confused and scared and wandering the woods alone."

93

"I doubt she's perplexed now. You see this dumb thing that this cult did? Well, it was a meager attempt at slowing her down, eventually killing her, and breaking the curse that had left the town safe, but it was quite unlucky for five families. If you check her chest, one of the four spirals is now gone, which means she is vulnerable. She must eat, or she will start to rot, and if they get hold of another spiral, it just worsens from there."

"So, you say she will kill over if they get all four? Like she was never upright and kicking?"

"Essentially, yes, but her mother is going to put up a hell of a fight, that I can assure you."

"Claire?" Now Andrew's gears were turning. Why didn't he see it before? Who else would have had the motive only to save one of the children? Who sent him here for more information that made her side look better than the other?

"Yes, and your little darling man-eater took the Scarlet Book; she wouldn't have thought to do so, which means that her mother is somehow physically connected to her body." Andrew knew that Mark was right; a few days ago, Andrew would have never believed it. He had seen a lot of things in his day, but all of this was entirely new to him. "So, you see, if Darla had all four energy sources, she would have made a complete recovery, but one of them was taken too soon, and I have no doubt they will go for the other three next, If not already."

"Lights out!" Hannah had been in lock up for a little less than two days and had already started to feel a little more like herself. It didn't stop her sadness that her family had died, but she was more than confident that she didn't have a thing to do with it. After a few hours of holding the day, she was arrested, she came down with the shakes, and then there was violent vomiting. Of course, the intake officers all thought she was just another junkie kid. In all reality, Hannah never had so much as smoked a cigarette or drank a beer, and she knew then, beyond any doubt, she had been drugged. She is more than likely to be framed for her family's murder, but why?

Hannah had noticed that two of the girls in holding with her seemed to take a genuine interest in whatever Hannah happened to be doing, and one of them never took their eyes off of her. It gave Hannah the creeps because she had heard some real horror stories about what went on in prison. Her lawyer had told her this evening that she had set up a hearing for Monday at one, and if all goes well, she should bail out since a few new pieces of evidence were brought to light. The girl knew she had to thank Hunter and Andrew because she wouldn't have stood a chance without them.

One of the two girls that took such an interest in Hannah, Belle, had been roomed up with another cell, but Willow, the bigger and tougher-looking one, was paired up in Hannah's cell. Hannah hated lights out because when the lights were off, all she could feel was Willow's cold Hazel eyes staring up from the bottom bunk, boring a hole into the back of Hannah's head. Willow rarely spoke, but tonight, after the guards left, the girl finally spoke up.

"Yo, Hannah," Willow whispered.

"Yeah?" Hannah asked; she tried as hard as she could not let the fear in her body come out in her words. "What do you want?"

"Are you a cold-blooded killer like everyone here says you are?" Hannah had to think for a second before she answered. She didn't want to say yes because it was a lie, but if she said no, it might make her a bigger target than she already was. What if her reputation was the only thing that kept them from fighting her...? Or worse.

"What if I said I was?" Hannah questioned and waited for Willow to answer. She could hear the girl roll over in the bunk below her. The springs were squeaky, probably from years of use.

"Well, if you said yes, it would make what I'm supposed to do much easier." A look of confusion crossed Hannah's face.

"What are you supposed to do?"

"Doesn't matter, but are you?" Again, Hannah thought, she couldn't bring herself to lie about something this serious, even if it meant getting her ass kicked in her cell.

"No, I don't think I am. Someone drugged me and killed my family. Hopefully, I will be out of here tomorrow, but you never know with the judicial system. Am I right?" Again, she could hear Willow at the bottom of the bunk. She could listen to the girl put her feet on the concrete floor and hear the springs squeak as Willow pulled something from under the mattress.

"Damn, that sucks," Willow said as she got to her feet.

"Why is that?" Hannah asked, confusion filling her voice. Willow grabbed the girl by the scruff of her jumper and pulled her to the ground. Hannah could hear her back slapping the concrete and feel the breath leave her lungs. Panic began to set in as she saw the shiv Willow had fashioned out of her old toothbrush. The girl came down fast and stabbed Hannah as hard as possible with the spike. When Hannah looked down, it was embedded in the palm of her left hand. Eyes widening, the air quickly returned, and she let out a scream that was soon muffled by one of Willow's hands.

"Shut the fuck up, Hannah, if you know what's good for you." Hannah's breathing became labored, but the girl swallowed another scream before it escaped her mouth. "I don't want to do this, probably as much as you don't want this done to you, but you're going to have to go with it, Hun. You can thank Claire Snead for all your pain and hardship and the fact that you had the nerve to date that girl, Susan. Yeah, you know, the one that offed herself all bloody like in the church a week ago. You didn't think we knew about that, did you? Yeah, we did." Hannah was beside herself with hate and fear for this girl. How did she know about Susan? They had kept it a secret. No one knew, and if Hannah's mother had ever found out about it, she would have gone crazy.

Taking her free hand, Willow grabbed the shiv and began to twist. Hannah couldn't help but a whimper; she could feel her warm blood pull into the palm of her hand and fall onto the dirty, cold floor. She knew she had to do something, but what? What could she do? After a few more twists, Willow let go of Hannah's mouth and removed the shiv from her palm. "There, was that so bad?" Hannah was frozen in fear and shock. Wasn't this psycho going to kill her? Why did she mangle her hand?

"But why? Why would you do this?" Hannah asked as she held up her bloody hand.

"You didn't know?" Willow asked as she walked over to the toilet and flushed the shiv. "A witch was draining your life force. An honest-to-God evil witch bitch. Ya know, you should be thanking me. If someone had heard us, I would have had to slit your ear to ear. I hate when shit like this gets messier than need be."

"A... Witch? Like Darla's mom? A witch?"

"Well fuck yes, what the hell did you think you and the boys were doing up in that old lady's apartment? Damn, I pegged you for many things, but stupid ain't one of em'." Willow walked back to her bunk and lay down. "I don't much care what you tell the guards, just leave me out of it, and if I were you, I would wash that out as best I can and see the nurse after breakfast; I sure hope you weren't a southpaw."

The drive back from Eagle's nest was a quiet one. Andrew had found Darla hiding in the trees on the right side of the house. Pretty close to where she had left Ethan's body. Andrew had offered to take Mark with them, but he assured the man that Zelda wouldn't have the guts to come back there a second time. Andrew still didn't want to leave the man there alone with a dead body on his front lawn, but Mark seemed unwavered by the carnage and again assured Drew that everything would take care of itself.

"You see," Mark explained, "I'm quite sure when this man tried to break into my house, he had a rather nasty head wound, and I remember in the paper, you understand... The masked assailant that broke into

Davis's house and stabbed him in yet another botched robbery was hit in the head with a baseball bat. He had also sustained a gunshot wound along the way. Could have been one of my neighbors, but the blood attracted a bear, and that's how he ended up in this unfortunate state." Andrew was helping Darla into the car's back seat but stopped to look at the small man, who now had a little grin.

"Do you think that will work? The bite marks on that man's body will not match a bear. I should know; I do this for a living."

"Unfortunately for the town's folk here at Eagle's nest, the police department will go along with whatever makes the paperwork end the fastest. You would be surprised at what you can get away with around here." Andrew nodded and got into the car to make his way home. Usually, his conscious mind would tell him that it was against the law and flat-out wrong to cover up a murder. The man on the front lawn in front of the Randolph residence, though, would have killed again and taken anyone he could with him. That he knew for sure, and to be perfectly honest, letting Councilperson Howards realize he had found and eliminated the threat towards his God son was a load off Drew's mind.

About two-thirds of the way home, Andrew began to notice Darla's erratic behavior beginning to return and couldn't help but become cautious of her actions. The last thing either of them needed was her attacking him while driving.

"Are you okay, Darla?" The girl looked at the man with soulless eyes and nodded. It was astonishing how quickly she healed after feeding off the man on the mountain.

"I do feel a bit strange," she said as she wrapped her arms around her waist. For the first time, Drew noticed the outline of a book under the girl's coat and motioned at it.

"What's that?" Drew asked, knowing full well what it was. Mark had mentioned it, but in the girl's frazzled state, Drew assumed she had lost it in the struggle.

"I'm not sure," Darla began, and she pulled the scarlet book from under her coat, handing it to Andrew. "Something in my head told me to take it. Told me not to let the bad lady steal it away. That it was important."

"Oh, I'm sure it is Darla. I think it might be time to talk to your mother about a few things. She's been up to something. I'm just not sure exactly how she's been doing it."

By the time they had gotten home, Darla had begun to get much worse, almost as if she had lost even more energy, and Andrew could see the blood lust in her eyes. There was no doubt that Mark was right about having to keep her locked away until she passed or she was cured.

Grabbing the girl by her wrists, Andrew struggled to open the front door. He found this hard to do, having the scarlet book safely tucked under one arm. Thankfully, Hunter came to his aide and opened the door, rushing them inside.

"Darla, you look... Better?" Hunter said in a confused haze. His entire day had been a dizzy haze, but he was glad that he had been able to prove Hannah's innocence, and with any luck, she would be released in the morning.

"We need to get her in a room and barricade it shut with whatever you have available," Andrew said with a look of fear in his eye. Hunter wanted answers but knew his best bet was to do what the man said. Pushing the girl into the guest bedroom, the two of them slammed the door shut and pushed the couch in front of it, essentially making the door impossible to open. The two flopped on the sofa and Drew handed Hunter the scarlet book.

"So, what did I miss?" Hunter asked, opening the book and beginning to read it to himself.

"Claire is definitely behind Darla's situation, and I am pretty confident that she is the one that has caused all this fuss with Matt and Hannah."

"You think she was the one that had those guys break in and hurt them? Who killed Hannah's family?" Hunter asked as he looked up at Drew for a second and then back at the book.

"No, not exactly. I think it's what she did to the kids that caused a chain reaction resulting in the death of the Whitcomb family and the attack on Davis and Matthew Dunbar. She somehow used them as a power source to keep her daughter upright and kicking."

"Well, that would make sense. Especially after what happened at Kelly's house today." Hunter said, barely taking his eyes off the book. It was absolutely fascinating. "I went there to talk to her about the bone saw. There was this guy there, Connor Biggs. Yeah, he confessed to the whole thing and implied that Kelly helped, and I already had suspicions about that. He's in custody and Finch Hollow Hospital."

"The hospital?" Andrew asked,

"Yeah, there was a bit of an altercation. I had to stab him. He should make a full recovery. So Hannah should be out of jail tomorrow. Her lawyer is meeting with her to discuss her release's specifics. No doubt she's going to need counseling."

"Well, that's two mysteries solved," Andrew muttered as he tried to look over Hunter's shoulder at the book.

"Two, you say?"

"Well, yes. Darla's condition worsened because her power sources were depleted, and she ate a guy at Mr. Randolph's. Hence the blood on her clothes. That helped her improve, but the guy she attacked had a

105

huge gash on his head. Best we can figure, he was the one that attacked the Dunbars, so he's out of the picture."

"Do we need to contact the police?" Hunter asked as he turned the page. They both could hear Darla scratching at the door. She had begun to make gasping and groaning sounds, and they both knew right away she was going feral again.

"No, Mark and I figured the Eagle's Nest police department would do an outstanding job of figuring that out. We have way too much on our plate as it is, Hunter." Hunter nodded in agreeance and shut the book for the night.

"I'm guessing we should give Claire a visit in the morning. I've checked our messages, and William Thurston is our shiny new missing person. My money is on Claire having something to do with it."

"How much you want to bet that if we look for Matthew, he would be conveniently missing as well," Drew said, rubbing his temples. If it weren't one thing, it was another, and if Chairperson Howards caught wind that his God son was again in mortal danger, there would be a lot of explaining.

"I have a rather clever idea about why you have this book too. Page 167 explains how to make a human power source. Kind of like replacing a dead battery. Almost like a soul transfer of sorts. It would kill the host but most likely restore Darla to full health." Hunter looked over at Drew, who looked right back at

Hunter. "I don't think this is such a cut-and-dry case, buddy. We aren't looking at good and bad; we have to decide what's the lesser of the two evils here." Andrew nodded and took off his hat, placing it between them.

"Zelda and her goons stopped by the Randolphs and essentially tried to kill us both. The body count is getting higher by the day. We better stop these crazy groups before there's no one left to save."

"I can't believe you did that! I explicitly told you NOT to go over there and interfere, but there you were all high and mighty, rolling into the station and shooting up the place like any of it would have ended well for the three of you. Just look at what happened to Ethan. LOOK!" Father Hall was pacing the length of his quarters, his hands were behind his back, and he had a look of fury on his face.

"You have to understand, Father, and he was trying to sabotage everything we were working for. He might have still ruined our plans. We were..." Hall's booming voice cut off Zelda.

"You were going in blind, and that's how things go south for us. We have the numbers, but not if you keep getting us all killed! Mr. Randolph is of no consequence to you. Do you understand?"

"Yes, sir," Zelda said as she stood to leave the room. Kevin was at her skirt tails, heading to the door when Father Hall noted one more thing.

"What would our leader think of you three? A waste of skin. The lot of you." His words stung her like a bee, but she didn't let him notice and just continued out of Father Hall's chambers and down to her own.

"We have to take that little historian down," Zelda mumbled under her breath.

"But father Hall said...." Zelda's mocking tone cut off Kevin.

"But Father Hall said, blah blah blah, he may be in charge of this place, but he isn't in charge of it all. That is for the beast to decide. I have spent my entire life here reading up on the coming of the beast, and it's nothing like you or Father Hall are thinking. The darkness isn't actually the darkness. It's the dwindling desires and hopes of all the people who doubt, and I will not have that darkness on my doorstep; no! I am going after Mark, and I will help brother Biggs escape his prison, and we will have our power, Kevin. If it's too much for you to oversee, that's alright. Why send a man to do a woman's job?" Zelda left Kevin in the hallway, and the man didn't know what to do. If he told on her, she would skin him alive. But if he didn't, something much worse might befall him.

With his head held low, he slowly walked back down the hall to Father Hall's quarters. He knew what he had to do, and he wasn't happy about it... Not one bit.

Hannah walked out of jail with her freedom. Her lawyer also had some other good news for the girl.

"Well, it looks like we have a gentleman that lives one town over who has graciously offered to let you stay with him until you have completed your counseling and can figure things out for yourself. Since you don't have any other next of kin." It was true that Hannah was essentially an orphan, and that thought hadn't crossed her mind in the last few days.

Once she had gathered her things and changed back into her clothes, her lawyer escorted her out of jail. Right at the gate, a small round man was standing beside a little blue car.

"Who is this?" Hannah asked, pointing at the man with his hands folded in front of his waste.

"That is Mr. Randolph. You will be staying with him for a little while. He lives over in Eagle's Nest. Nice person. Town historian. He used to do this quite well in his youth, so we already had his background check and stuff in the system." Hannah's lawyer put his hand on her shoulder and looked the girl in the eye. "If you think things are going south, you have my number, but there was no one else, Hannah... No one." Hannah nodded, and without another word, the girl walked over to the man and silently got into the back of the car.

The drive up the mountain was quiet initially, but Mark couldn't manage the silence.

"I'm sure you know; my name is Mark Randolph. I hope you will find my cabin to your liking. We have many spare rooms, and you can have anyone that suits your fancy."

"We? Does someone else live with you?" Hannah asked as she looked out of the window. The first snow of the fall must have hit the mountain faster than in Finch Hollow. She could see the glistening tree branches dancing in the wind like chandelier glass. The scenery was breathtaking, and she hadn't been out of Finch Hollow long. She assumed she should make the best of a dire situation and be grateful to the little man for allowing her to have a roof over her head and food to eat. With any luck, she would get to finish her senior year of high school and get the hell out of dodge.

"Not exactly, but I tend to have visitors from time to time, and I might be expecting one or two in the following days if everything pans out the way I'm thinking. Either way, you're always welcome here." Pulling up to the three-story cabin, Hannah's eyes became more prominent than saucers. She had never seen anything as magnificent as what stood before her.

"Oh my God, is this yours?" Hannah asked. Mark laughed a little and put the car in park.

"Well, last time I checked, it was. If you like to read, I also have a huge library in the back on the first floor, but I do have to warn you, it's mostly history stuff. I do love my job, after all." Hannah nodded and got out of the car. Looking over at the front door, she thought she could make out something red on the ground.

"What's that?" She asked, pointing to the big red spot by the front door.

"Oh, this old girl here got a transmission leak. Took me hours to spray down. That spot might be icy; make sure you don't step over there." Walking to the front door, Mark fidgeted with his keys and unlocked the top lock. He pushed the door open and motioned for her to enter.

The rest of the day was spent letting Hannah get settled in. She was surprised at how well she and Mark got along, and they spent hours joking and talking about happy memories. At dinner, though, the conversation went in a different direction.

"I'm so glad you could get out of jail. The thought that you could have done anything like that baffles the imagination. I am pleased you feel at home here in this big musty cabin." Hannah nodded and took a big bite of her pork chop. It might have been the jail food, or it might have been from the sheer enjoyment of freedom, but that might have been the most delicious pork chop she had ever put into her mouth.

"I should be thanking you, Mr. Randolph. My lawyer told me that no one else came up to offer to help. Without you, I would have been in one of those halfway houses. I couldn't imagine how that would have been." Mark nodded and took a few bites of his food before continuing his conversation.

"Well, it wasn't just out of the goodness of my heart that I offered to let you stay here. I may have had a few more selfish reasons for the invitation."

"Really, what do you mean?" Hannah asked, she knew there had to be a catch, and the sound of what he had said, put her a little on edge.

"It's nothing terrible, Hannah, I promise, but it has something to do with what happened to you and your parents." Pointing over at her hand, the man motioned at her injury. "I see that someone has

114

already done what I had feared was going to happen in jail." Hannah put down her fork and knife and nodded at the man.

"What do you know about the girl who attacked me?" Hannah asked, she didn't want to come off as cold, but she had to understand why anyone would want to cut her hand open and leave her there with no attempt at murder or explanation.

"To be honest with you, not a lot, but many weird things are going on around here lately. Hannah and I want to make sure that you are safe for the time being. At least until the killers are all behind bars and things can get back to normal."

"I heard they had someone in custody."

"Oh, they do, but I'm sure he didn't act alone. In fact, I'm quite certain he had a few people pulling his strings. Here you can have anything your heart desires, but you cannot leave the house for any reason. Is that clear?" Hannah nodded and picked her fork up once again to eat. "I have everything arranged, your counseling will be in the home, and your schoolwork will be done remotely. Just let me know if you want a friend over, and I will send a car to fetch them." Again, Hannah nodded, she wasn't sure exactly why the man was so protective of her, but at the end of the day, it was oddly comforting to know someone out there cared.

Hunter and Andrew had walked up to the old apartment building, book in hand. They both knew that Claire wouldn't have let them in otherwise. Pushing the doorbell, Hunter stayed out of the camera; he wanted to ensure that when Claire looked at her monitor, she would have a clear view of the book. After a few moments, Claire's voice rang over the intercom.

"Andrew, why do I have the pleasure of you gracing me once more with your presence?" Andrew smirked and looked up at the monitor.

"I've thought of a few more questions to which you may have the answers. Might we come up and talk for a while?" There was a brief silence on the other side of the monitor and then a beep, unlocking the front door for the two men to enter.

Hunter looked around at the old Hotel in awe. It was magnificent. Following his comrade up the steps to Claire's door, for the first time in a while, Hunter felt the pang of nervousness bubble up from his stomach into his chest. He always knew when he had that gut reaction to watch his back. He knew Ms. Snead was up to no good, but he wasn't sure what she had up her sleeve.

Opening the door, Claire motioned for them to sit down on the couch, and she took the chair on the other side of the room.

"What can I do for you two, fine gentlemen, this evening?" She had a cup of steaming hot tea sitting in front of her, but it didn't smell quite right to Hunter. "Oh, how rude of me. Can I get either of you a nice cup of herbal tea? I just made it a few minutes ago; it was almost like I knew you were coming." Claire let out a little laugh, and again, it didn't sound quite right to Hunter.

"Ms. Snead, we have researched your story, you know, the one that you told me on our last visit, and even though there were a few discrepancies in your variation and Mr. Randolph's, you may have hit the nail on the head."

"Well, what did I tell you, Mr. Bower? When you're in the know, you're usually right." Andrew put the scarlet book gently on his lap and continued to stare at Claire with intent in his eyes.

"All these smoke and mirror divergence, it isn't who we are, Ms. Snead."

"Claire, you can call me Claire." She said, picking up her cup of tea. "Smoke and mirrors, you say?"

"We know you know that we have your daughter."

"Well, I should hope so; she was brought to your morgue after all." Claire took a sip of her tea and listened with mock interest as Andrew continued.

"You know what I mean... Claire. She's up and mobile, and you also know there is no natural reasoning. We also know you had something to do with it." Claire let out a little snicker and put her cup back onto the table.

"Are you feeling quite well, Mr. Bower? What you're saying makes me sound like some ... of which or something. How on Earth would I have anything to do with my daughter's living? She died last week, and now you're mocking her death?" Claire began to get out of her seat to tell the men to go, but Hunter raised a hand.

"You know how, and I'm pretty sure you know the two boys that have gone missing, Matthew and William, and I think you had something to do with it." This time the woman's brow furrowed, and she slowly sat back down in her chair.

"What's that?" she asked as she pointed to the scarlet book.

"Oh, this thing?" Andrew asked as he held the book up in front of him. "It would seem that your daughter snagged it from Mr. Randolph's library, looks like there is a spell in here that can bring her back one hundred percent, just one little catch; it costs a living soul. So, which one of the lucky boys were you planning on murdering?"

"You don't understand...." Claire was cut off by Hunter, who had gotten to his feet.

"No, you don't understand. You can't just go around killing people. There is no good reason to do that. I am sorry for what happened to your daughter. I wouldn't wish that on anyone, but she's dead, and you must let dead things lie." Getting to her feet, the woman was now in full-on anger mode.

"How dare you!" She screamed as she ran at Hunter, who held his hands up in self-defense. He thought she was going to attack him but instead ran into the kitchen and came back out with a butcher knife. "I will kill both of you right where you stand!" she screamed. Now both the men were standing side by side, and Andrew had put the scarlet book on the coffee table. Lunging at Hunter, the woman tried her best to slide the blade into the man's chest, but he managed to grab the blade; when she pulled back, the sharp knife sliced deeply into the palms of Hunter's hands. With a scream of pain, the man retreated, holding both hands together like she was praying.

"We can talk about this, Claire," Andrew said, but before he knew it, she had the man on the floor with the knife over his head aimed at his right eye. She was pushing down hard, but Andrew was stronger, holding her hands and the blade just a few inches from his face. "Claire, please." Hunter had already begun to feel dizzy from the blood loss but could tell that his friend was in trouble. Attempting to walk over to his aide, he hit the table with his knee, knocking over the cup of tea and its contents.

"NO!" Claire shouted but didn't let up on the knife in front of Andrew's face. It was almost as if the spilled tea had given the woman renewed strength. Letting out a battle cry, Hunter lunged at the woman, and she fell off Andrew, who quickly got to his feet. Hunter had Claire in a reverse bear hug, but she pushed back on the man, and they both fell to the floor. The two barrels rolled across the floor a few times before all the action abruptly stopped. Hunter was on top of Claire, and Claire lay belly down on the dense wood floor. It was a few moments before Hunter realized the blood under her wasn't just his, and he jumped to his feet in fright.

"What happened!" Hunter exclaimed; Andrew could hear the fear in his voice. Leaning over, Andrew rolled the woman over. The knife had lodged itself into the base of her neck, and by the looks of it, given the length and width, there was a good chance it had pierced her brain on impact.

Because of all the action that had so abruptly started, the men didn't realize the tea had spilled and had made its way to the scarlet book, and it wasn't until Andrew heard the moaning from the other room it hadn't even occurred to him that there might have been someone else there. Putting a finger up his lips, he motioned for Hunter to stay where he was. Making his way to the far-left corner door of the apartment, Andrew turned the knob and let it creak open. A look of relief washed across the man's face.

"We found them," Andrew said. "Matt and Will, we found them."

Officer Jenkins sat outside of the local sheriff's door and pondered over the case file in his hands. He had been waiting for quite some time to bend Andrew's ear about a few things that had baffled him in that little manila folder. The crime-fighting duo had managed to find the missing teens, but in doing so, put a knife in Claire Snead, which threw a wrench in the man's plans of talking to her. In any case, it was a good save on their end, and Chairperson Howards had already wandered out of his fancy condominium to hold a brief press conference mere hours after the discovery. Howards had sung the two men's praises and kept them in the highest regard for saving his godson and William Dunbar.

Jenkins could hear the three men on the other side of the door talking among themselves and the stenographer typing away as they did so in hushed urgency. He was about to give up and go home when the entrance to the office opened, and the men emerged from the room.

"We want to thank you again, Mr. Bower, Mr. William, for finding those boys, and even though they weren't in one hundred percent condition, they are both deemed to have a full recovery... That is if William Dunbar comes out of his coma." The three of them shook hands, and the Sheriff retired to his room to start on the paperwork, which would probably take him the rest of the night.

"Andrew," Officer Jenkins said as he got to his feet. "I've been trying to contact you all day. You're a hard man to contact these days."

"I'm so sorry, Jenkins," Andrew said as he turned to face the man. He could see the tiredness on the officer's face, and it aged him a few years since he saw him last. No, this wasn't a job for the weak-hearted, whom Andrew knew firsthand, absentmindedly reaching up and touching the widow's peak under his fedora. "What can we do for you?"

"I thought you should be the first, well, the second set of eyes to look at what your crack partner picked up on the Whitcomb case while you were pounding the pavement." Officer Jenkins handed the folder to the men, and they both opened it looking intently at the pages that contained everything else the man had tried to piece together.

"So, it looks like that sample I took from the Whitcomb's, which couldn't be from old' Mr. Biggs," Hunter said as he pointed to the paper. Andrew nodded and looked up at officer Jenkins.

"It looks like this might put the final nail in her coffin," Andrew said, turning the page.

"What does that mean?" Jenkins asked, scratching his head.

"More than likely, the woman that was scratched the night of the murder wasn't Hannah Whitcomb, even though we can get a DNA sample to rule her out; no, I'm pretty sure the girl you're looking for is Kelly Hartfield." Hunter mused as he began to look even more intently at the second page.

"Kelly Hartfield? The one who works on the north nurse's station?" Jenkins asked.

"The one and only, and also the one who was just wanted for harboring a fugitive until Connor's trial date is set. We had one of your guys do a background check on Mr. Biggs, and he was no choir boy; let's just put it that way, shall we." Hunter's eyes widened, and he pointed at the next thing on the page that delighted him. "I knew it!"

"What!" Jenkins was starting to get a little flustered at all the cryptic talking. Andrew shut the folder and handed it back to Officer Jenkins.

"It would seem as though there was another person in that house the night of the killing, and as if the confession weren't enough, made sure you see what side shoe Mr. Biggs wears, my money is eleven and a half. Secondly, the food was drugged, Olanzapine. Causes drowsiness and hallucinations. Find Kelly and talk to Doctor Winters; I also think one of his prescription pads might be missing." Officer Jenkins nodded and gave both of the men his award-winning smile.

"You know, I would have thought the two of you would have been more shaken up, seeing as Claire died before you both."

"Well," Hunter held up his bandaged hands, "I did get this little parting gift, and she wasn't exactly the nicest of people. Not to mention, we come face to face with death on the daily."

Dr. Winters walked into the ICU wearing his white lab coat, looking as professional as he could. Zelda had told him that she would have made Kelly do it, but the girl was in hiding and needed a slightly more important task that couldn't take place unless phase one was completed. Doctor Winters didn't complain; he was one of the few in the group who had signed up for the task. Being a doctor, he got to hold people's lives in his hands, and he had let a few falls to the floor, shattering lives in the process, and hardly ever felt bad about it. To say the man had a God complex was putting it mildly, and the nurses here had experienced the worst side of Doctor Winters, Kelly included.

Walking to William's bedside, the man picked up the metal folder. He opened it and pretended to care about the information inside, but just long enough for anyone walking by the open the door to assume he was checking in on a patient. It was amusing to the man that William's best friend was right across the hall asleep, with a belly full of food, and well, Will here, he lost the love of his life, the use of his body, and quite possibly his mind if that thing inside of him had taken too much of his energy and that was also why Dr. Winters thought what he was doing was also quite noble in a way.

Pulling the scalpel out of his left side pocket, the man made a small incision into Will's left hand; opening it just slightly, he pulled a small shiny spiral from the boy's palm.

"There you go, son. Two stitches, and you will be done." Pulling the needle and thread from his right pocket, the man had William sewn up in less than three minutes. He knew he would have to leave soon because when Darla took her last breath, William would wake up, and so would the Beast. Leaving the ICU, Dr. Winters felt a cold chill go down his spine. He couldn't decide whether that was Darla's end or the evening's excitement. Either way, the man would spend the rest of the night revisiting this moment. The moment he finished what the others couldn't and the evening, it all started to come together. No one could stop the prophecy, and anyone that stood in the Beast's way would surlily suffer and parish; if not for the Beast's hands, his followers weren't scared to do what had to be done.

Drew and Hunter finally made it home. It had felt like they had spent more time driving or at the morgue than in the quiet space of their dwelling. This bothered Andrew more because he hadn't seen his apartment in days. Throwing their coats on the couch in front of the guest bedroom door, the two looked at each other.

"Should we?" Hunter couldn't finish his sentence because Andrew had already begun to shake his head no. "But we can't leave her starving, Drew!" Hunter crossed his arms and looked over at the man, who had taken off his hat and sat on the couch. Scratching his temple, he thought for a second.

"No, you're right. Even though the girl in the other room is technically dead, we should give her some food. Wait, did that sound as weird to you as it did to me?" Hunter smirked and picked up the phone.

"Well, since our dead girl already ate me out of house and home, I thought we could go in a slightly other direction and order pizza. I'm sure a piece would fit under the door, if nothing else. One can hold the door shut while the other feeds Darla."

"Sounds like a plan," Andrew said. Two pies were on their way when they began noticing the apartment's lack of noise.

"Why can't I hear her in there?" Hunter asked as he looked back at the door.

"I would have commented on the smell a while ago, but I know how she gets when she starts to get run down. You don't think...."

"No," Hunter began, "I would have figured Will would have had one more charge in him... You don't think killing Claire would of...."

"No, I mean...." Andrew and Hunter became as quiet as a mouse. They waited for what felt like forever. They thought they knew what to do, and neither one was incredibly happy about it.

"Alright, fine." Hunter began as they both got up off the couch, "A quick in and out."

"You don't have to remind me, Hunter; I was there when she tore a man to shreds; I'm good." Grabbing either side of the couch, the two slid it away from the door. Andrew leaned into the door and listened for signs of life but couldn't hear a thing. He shook his head and opened the door.

With a creak, the door opened, and the two of them popped their heads into the opening. There, on the floor, lying face down, was Darla. She had looked almost delicate when they had put her in there a few hours ago, but now she reminded Hunter of a body that had been out in the elements for about a week, and the smell lingered in his nose to prove his point.

"Oh my God," Andrew said as he covered his mouth and nose. "I'm used to the smell, but the potency is strangulating. Hunter nodded in agreeance as he took a cautionary step inside the room. Every minute or so, he thought he could make out Darla's chest heave up and then back down almost as if in an attempt to continue breathing, but Hunter convinced himself that it was just his imagination.

"What do we do now?" Hunter asked; he couldn't take his eyes off the body on the floor, he was still a zombie movie fanatic, and he knew he had to be better safe than sorry. Andrew shrugged and motioned for Hunter to back away from Darla.

"We must get her back to the morgue and prep her for cremation. There is no way that we can have an open casket... Not like that." Hunter took another step forward and reached down slightly with a bandaged hand but jerked it back quick as lightning when the doorbell rang. "It's probably the pizza."

Andrew said with a snort and walked toward the front door leaving Hunter in the room alone.

A little, pimple-faced teenage boy was on the other side of the door. Andrew could tell he had most likely just gotten his car and license.

"That'll be...." The boy pulled the paper out of his heat bag to double-check the cost. Twenty-four fifty." Andrew nodded and sifted around in his pockets.

"Give me a second; I think I left my wallet in the kitchen." The boy nodded and began to sniff the air like a bloodhound.

"Yo, did a raccoon die in one of your walls too? Cause your place smells like my buddy Mitchell's, a raccoon died in his chimney. It took like a week to get that thing out of there."

"Uh, yeah. That's exactly what happened. Sorry for the smell." Andrew yelled from the kitchen.

Meanwhile, Hunter had finally gathered enough courage to roll the girl on her back. Her eyes had popped out of her head, and the wound that had all but healed a few hours before had now returned and consumed most of the contents of her skull. Her tongue had swollen, and her skin had begun to blister around her mouth.

"This is both remarkable and horrifying all at the same time," Hunter said to himself; he scratched his head and felt a little trickle of blood, warm and wet, fall onto his cheek. Looking at his hand, he realized that he must have popped a stitch when he had messed with Darla's corpse. Absentmindedly he held his hand out to investigate, and in doing so, he accidentally let a drop or two falls onto Darla's face. That was all she needed to sit up at attention. She let out a gurgled moan, and Hunter let out a high-pitched scream that echoed through the house.

"Hey, what was that?" The pizza boy asked as Andrew returned to the front door with thirty dollars.

"Um, we have the...." Andrew was cut off by Hunter and Darla, arm in arm, falling from the bedroom door, knocking an old picture from the wall and shattering it to pieces on the floor. The boy's eyes widened, and a look of shock crossed his face. "Look, we can explain."

"Wow, that is the best Cosplay I've ever seen! Like EVER!" The boy mused. Handing the pizza boy his money and taking the pizza while pure chaos was going on behind him, Andrew just smiled, nodded, and shut the door.

Running to his friend's side and throwing the food on the couch as he passed it, Andrew managed to pull the girl off Hunter. She had already begun to lose steam, and within a few minutes, she was back on the floor in a stinky lump.

"What the Hell happened?" Andrew asked in a huff.

"I popped a stitch, and a few drops fell on her. I thought she was dead, but she was mostly dead."

"Well, one thing is for sure, we gotta get her to the morgue and keep anything blood-related away from her until she's set for cremation."

One thing that the whole town missed that night was right on the outskirts of town in a little out-of-the-way field. Across that field was a mountain, and a tiny town called a Coral boy was on the other side of the hill. Many peculiar and unexplained things liked to happen there, and Finch Hollow had heard a boatload of them. Most of the people in the Hollow wouldn't dare to venture that close to Coral Bay, and that is precisely why what happened there was unseen by human eyes.

The mountain moved. Yes, it moved ever so slightly, and even if someone out there had seen it, they might have written it off as a hallucination, but then something else happened. This one would have been almost impossible to write off. A door appeared at the base of the mountain. This door was unextraordinary, except that it just appeared out of nowhere. It was tan and had a plain brass handle rigidly attached to the right side of it. No frame what, so ever could be seen on its edges.

The door opened, and out stepped a tall thin man wearing an ash-grey suit and holding a briefcase. He straightened his tie and fixed his thick black-framed glasses before stepping through the threshold and onto the dewy grass of the field. The door shut behind him but didn't disappear. Looking around him, the man smiled and looked at his gold watch before walking straight across the field and into town. He had much work to do, and because of the work of a few meddling humans, he had been pushed back almost a whole week. No, that would not do for him. Now he had to rush what could have been something much more entertaining.

Kelly had to wait until after hours to get the new card from Dr. Winters. She had already attempted to get into the hospital once using her old key card, but the police were everywhere, and she knew she wouldn't be doing Connor any favors if she got caught. She was his only hope of getting out of there with his skin. He should have killed Hunter when he had the chance, now they were both on the run, and Kelly wouldn't go out without a fight. She couldn't go back to jail. That life was not for her.

Once she got to the west wing ICU, she could see that they had stationed a police officer at the door, but that was soon taken care of when Dr. Winters walked up to him and said something in a hushed tone. Kelly didn't care what the Doctor said because it seemed to strike the officer's attention, and he followed Winters down the hall and around the corner.

Kelly slipped down the hall and into the room. Connor hadn't noticed; he had been too busy fishing around in a bowl of green jello. Kelly fell behind a dividing sheet only to be met with Davis Dunbar. Kelly covered her mouth to hold back the squeak from her throat.

She knew that Ethan and others from the group had stabbed the man, which was not part of the plan. Davis was asleep. She didn't want to wake him. Popping her head out from the curtain, Kelly watched as a tall thin man with a grey suit and tied made his way into the room. She thought for a moment that the group may have hired someone for Connor's defense, but she had never seen him before, and there posed the question, who was this guy?

Connor Biggs?" The man asked. Connor looked up at the man and was unimpressed.

"Yeah? What do you want?" Connor asked as he finally gave up on the jello and focused all his attention on the man standing over him.

"Ah, good. I believe you are first on my list of people to meet." The man turned around, put his briefcase on the chair by the door, and popped the latches.

"Are you a lawyer or something? Did Father Hall send for you?" Connor was becoming increasingly confused as he took the man in. There was nothing special about him, and he was almost forgettable. What could a man like that want with Connor Biggs? The most unforgettable man in town.

"My name is Norman Beast, and I am an auditor. See, I audit who is useful to me and who is not."

"Norman... Beast? As in The Beast?" Connor let out a snorted laugh and slapped his leg. This caused his wound to become sore, but he couldn't help himself. Either this man is joking, or the whole group has been duped.

"There is no way that you are who you say you are... None. Sir, the Beast is a monster and a king, and you are...." Connor waved his hand up and down, "Whatever this is." Norman gave the man no attention and was unphased at Connor's actions. He took a piece of paper from his case and looked it over.

"You would be quite surprised at what can hide inside a simple shell. Never you mind at what I look like, Mr. Biggs." Norman looked over the paper in his hand and adjusted his glasses again. Kelly couldn't understand what she was hearing. This thin man couldn't possibly be who he said he was. Who was he? What was he doing? "Ah yes, it would seem that your use to me has ended; you have nothing more to give."

"Now, that can't be right. I killed a whole family for you! It was the three sacrifices written in the old texts. It was supposed to ensure power." The Beast snickered.

"Oh, how I do love those vague scriptures. No one ever reads the fine print. It almost always works in my favor. Yes, it does ensure power, Mr. Biggs, but it never said who gets it, and, to be frank, you don't deserve the skin your living in." Norman grabbed the paper and ripped it in half, and as he did so, Connor's skin tore away from his flesh.

Kelly's eyes widened as she let out a scream that lit up the room, but it was outmatched by Connor's screams of panic and pain. "I'm a beast, Mr. Biggs, but I'm no monster, so I will put you out of your misery now instead of letting you go into shock. Snapping his fingers, Connor lit up like he had been showering in Gas; Kelly let out another scream, and Davis jolted awake.

"What... What's going on?" He spoke. Kelly put her hand over his mouth and pulled him out of bed.

"We must go; we have to get out of here." Pulling the man to his feet, they made their way to the hallway door.

"You don't have to rush Kelly Hartfield, you're on my list, but I have a few other audits to deal with first. Just know I could kill you where you stand right now if I deem it so." The sound of the man's voice put a chill on her skin, and the smell of sulfur and burning flesh filled her nostrils, but the two of them managed to leave the room and make it out into the parking lot before the fire alarms were sounded. Putting Mr. Dunbar in Connor's old white truck, the two drove off into the night. She knew she had to find Hunter, tell him that the beast had returned to Finch Hollow, and tell him that she was marked for death. If there were any way around this, he would find it. But if not, darkness would fall on this town.

Under cover of night, Zelda had slipped out of the old church and made her way back to Eagles Nest. She went up to the top of the mountain and finished what she had started with Mark Randolph. The man had been expecting her, so when she strolled up to the front door. He had already unlocked it. Stepping into the house, she made her way back to his conservatory, where he always sat to smoke, and she could smell his pipe wafting in from the back. Mark thought he looked regal, but Zelda always thought the tiny man looked like a weathered sea captain.

"What took you so long, Zelda? I would have figured you would have been here hours ago." Mark gave the woman a cold stare as he took another puff off his pipe.

"There were some loose ends to tie up at the church. You know how things can be."

"Indeed, I do. The power struggle is great at the moment. You, for example, want it all for yourself." Zelda smirked at the old man. But he was right; Zelda did want all the power for herself. Who wouldn't?

Hannah was jarred awake by the conversation on the floor below her. She thought about staying in her room, but curiosity got the better of her, and she ventured out into the hallway and down a few steps to eavesdrop on Mark and the woman. She could make them out between the banister rails and hold them with both hands, pushing her face against the wood to get a better view.

"I thought you should know your little plan didn't work out as you had intended. The boys didn't take the bait. They ended up killing the witch and her daughter. The beast is walking amongst us, and I have no doubt he will be making his way here soon." Mark took another puff of his pipe before sitting it in front of him in an ashtray on the wooden table.

"I certainly hope so, after all the work I've put into his arrival. I've even prepared a room for him right above us, complete with the Innocent." The woman scoffed at the man's comment.

"What on Earth do you even mean? He will surely devour you for betraying him the way you did." More than ever, Hannah was more interested in what the two of them were saying. What was the innocent? Was he talking about her? Mark got to his feet and walked around the table; standing right in front of Zelda, he held his stare.

"You are quite stupid, aren't you, Zel? You can't seem to look past the obvious and get the whole picture. When I say I am on my side of things, that's exactly what I mean. I wanted them to get the book; I knew that their good-natured ways would end badly. They couldn't even bring themselves to kill a girl who was already dead. No, they are little do-righters, and I had them in my pocket from the start. I have people that work for me that don't even know they work for me." Zelda's eyes squinted as she took a step closer.

"I'm not sure what that is supposed to mean, Mark, but one thing is for sure." Zelda pulled the gun from her right front pocket and held it at the man's head. "I'm not leaving here tonight without finishing what I started last time." Mark let out a huge bellowing laugh straight from the gut.

"What are you going to do with that thing?" Mark mused as he leaned one hand on the wooden table behind him.

"I don't care what father Hall says. You're a liability, and you need to be eliminated."

"It would seem like we have found someone smarter than you, Zelda. He works for ME, not you. Hell, you work for me too." Lifting his hand, the man waved Zelda away. Something was happening to her, and she couldn't quite figure out what, but when she tried to pull the trigger, she couldn't.

"What's happening?" Zelda said; she could feel the fear rise from her throat as the realization hit her; she was now pointing the gun at herself.

"I would have done this the last time you were here, but I had to make it look realistic... Well realistic enough to convince Andrew that we were on the same side. I am the one pulling the strings, darling... You are my puppet. You all are." With that, he manufactured another gesture with his hand, and Zelda pulled the trigger blowing half of her head off. Dropping the gun to the floor, the woman stood there for a second before killing in front of Mark. Hannah let out a scream moments later, taking the grin off the man's face.

"Oh my, Hannah dear, call 911; Zelda has committed suicide!"

William finally awoke the following day. He had quickly heard about the tragic fire that had killed Connor Biggs in the room down the hall. He had also heard about the disappearance of Matt's father and that Kelly was on the run from the law in connection with the murders of the Whitcomb family.

"Dang, you fall asleep for a few days, and the whole town gets flipped on its side," William said as he took another large bite of his chicken noodle soup.

"You can say that again." Doctor Winters said, looking over the boy's chart. "Well, the good news is that you can go home tomorrow. Your mother should be thrilled."

"I don't know why Claire would have done what she did to me. What did she have to gain from drugging us and locking us away?" William was asking this question more to himself than to the doctor.

"I know she was still grieving the loss of her daughter, and grief can make you do weird things." Doctor Winters left the room without saying another word.

A few minutes later, there was a knock on the door, and Matt walked in, holding his IV bag in his good hand.

"Yo, bro, you finally woke up! I've been waiting for you, man." William smiled up at Matt. It was good to see him. At this point, he almost felt like Matthew was the only friend he had in the world.

"What's up?" Will said as he took another bite of his lunch.

"What's up? We have to get out of here. We gotta find my dad and stop what's happening." William gave Matthew an odd look and tilted his head to the side.

"I know a lot of weird shit has gone down this week, but I don't think either one of us should be going anywhere. We were drugged and left for dead in that apartment. They still don't know what kind of drug it was." Matthew walked over to William's bed and looked sternly at the boy.

"We weren't drugged; Claire was a witch." William snorted, laughed, and took another spoonful of soup.

"Sure, that math adds up." William rolled his eyes, but Matthew was unamused. Grabbing the spoon from Will, he looked down at the boy, and the sternness in his eyes got even more intense.

"I'm serious, Will. I don't know how I know some of these things I do. Like how I know the guy in the room that caught fire, well, he's in some cult thing, and now that Claire is gone, this other guy is roaming the halls of this hospital killing. We are not safe here, and my dad might be in trouble. So get your clothes on, and I will meet you back here in half an hour."

"You don't think they will let us walk out of here, do you? There are people everywhere." Matt looked over at Will and smiled.

"We are going to use that to our advantage." Half an hour later, they were dressed and walking down the hallway. It almost seemed as if no one was going to stop them until they hit the west wing nurses' station, and one of the staff asked them where they were going.

"Oh, um, well, I don't quite...." William began to stutter, but Matt could see the exit a few yards away and took the opportunity to push the nurse down. Grabbing his friend's hand, the two tore down the hall and out into the sunlight of a brisk fall day.

"Where are we going?" William asked.

"I don't know," Matthew responded as the two of them continued to run across the Parking lot. "But I think I may know someone who will have some answers for us."

Father Hall had finally lost his cool when Kevin entered his chambers for the second time that evening. Kevin told the man about Zelda's plans to kill Mark and how she told Kevin that she didn't care about what Father Hall had said.

"She must be stopped by any means necessary!" Father Hall screamed. "Mark Randolph must be kept alive."

"I couldn't agree more." A voice called from the church's hallway. The two men turned around to see a tall thin man in a grey suit holding a briefcase standing in the doorway.

"Who the hell are you?" Father Hall hissed.

"I have always enjoyed that turn of phrase Father, especially from a person of the cloth... Although we both know that's just a costume. This is a way to sucker this town to get what you want. I like that in a man." Norman walked over to Father Hall's desk and put down the case, popping the latches and opening it. He pulled out a piece of paper and looked it over. "In any case, I am here for one, Kevin Underwood."

"Um, that's me. What is this about?" Kevin had never seen the man before in his life. He looked like a lawyer or someone who would do your taxes in a well-fitted suit. Norman fidgeted with his glasses as he looked the paper over in his hand.

"I do apologize for the delay in returning. That witch and her offspring refusing to die was the matter." Kevin's eyes widened as he looked the man over once more. Was there something there that he didn't see before? No, there was no way this man could be who he said he was. "My name is Norman Beast. I am the auditor."

"Your no beast. You..." Father Hall looked over his shoulder at the mirror by the door, and his mouth almost fell to the floor. Norman's reflection did not match his appearance. It was the opposite of unremarkable. Norman was a creature of the pits with brown scales covering his entire head; he had one rather large horn at the top that split into two at the very tip. Yes, he still wore the grey suit, but he was much, MUCH larger than Father Hall was expecting. "Oh my, you, your...." Father Hall couldn't finish his sentence or stop looking at the reflection on the other side of the room.

"it says here that you, Kevin, have been with the group for the last six years. There is this tiny little blemish on your record, though. We cannot overlook the attempted murder of one Mark Randolph."

"Hey, now!" Kevin started, "You can't blame that on me! It was all Zelda's idea! She's up there right now trying to do it again!"

"I wouldn't worry too much about that, Kevin," Norman said, smiling a little. His smile was almost as unremarkable as everything else the man standing in front of Kevin had to be seen. "He's had enough of the ladies' shenanigans and offed her. He is quite a go-getter, that man." Kevin's mouth shut as he looked down at the ground. "The one thing that my paper hadn't stated was exactly how much of a tattle tale you are. Is this a new bad habit you've begun to exhibit? Well, in any case, you're of no use to me." Norman crinkled the paper in his hand, and Father Hall began to hear a cracking sound as he did so. He tore his eyes away from the reflection and over to Kevin screaming in pain, lying on the floor in a twisted bundle. Every bone in the man's body was bent in abnormal shapes; some had begun to rip through the flesh and poke out, splintering and popping like kindling in a fire.

"I'm a beast, Kevin, but I'm no monster, and because of that, I am going to put you out of your misery now." Dropping the bundle of paper on the

153

floor, Mr. Beast stomped it with his foot, and as soon as the paper smashed, so did Kevin's head, almost as if someone had put a grenade inside his brain. Bone and grey matter scatter the room. Father Hall stared in awe at the man in front of him. He had never been in the presence of such power before. He was both honored and horrified.

"What... What about me, Mr. Beast." Again, the man smiled and looked down into his briefcase. Pulling out a paper, he began to look it over.

"Ah yes, Father Frances Hall, it would seem that you have some beneficial skills, one of them being influence over this little town. I think I'm going to enjoy collaborating with you." With a snap of the Beast's fingers, Father Hall's paper went up in smoke. Hall squinted, believing he would go up in flames with the paper, but nothing happened, and when he opened his eyes, the man had vanished, leaving Kevin's crumpled and lifeless body on the floor as a keepsake. He couldn't help but wonder what the Beast had in store for him; sitting down in his chair, he threw a fist down on his table. It wasn't challenging, he thought, but Norman had left more than carnage as a gift.

Lifting his hand from the table, Father Hall saw that he had made a crack in the wood, a rather large gap, and he smiled. The Beast had given him power, just like he had promised, and now Father Hall had more than words to back up his beliefs.

Kelly and Davis had sat outside Hunter's house all night. She couldn't imagine what he had gotten himself into that would have kept him away for so long. At some point during the night, they both had fallen asleep, but at the sun's first light, Kelly was woken up by the screeching sound of Andrew's old yellow beater.

"Hey, Davis, they are back," Kelly said, shaking the man awake. Davis moaned a little and rubbed his eyes. The pain medication they had given him had begun to wear off, and the throbbing in his side had worsened over the last few hours. Looking around the road to ensure no one else was around, the two hurried across the street and met Drew and Hunter on the front stoop.

"Kelly?" Hunter asked as he opened the front door. The woman ushered the three men into the house and shut the door behind them.

"The cops are looking for you. What do you think will stop me from calling them right now and turning you in?" Andrew said in a huff as he reached into his pocket for his phone and quickly realized that he had left it in the car... Again.

"You have to listen to us. We are all in some serious shit. The beast is already here." Davis began to sniff the air and make a weird face.

"What is that smell?" Davis asked as he sat down on the couch.

"A raccoon died in the chimney," Andrew said. Davis looked around the house and scratched his head.

"You don't have a chimney."

"Yeah, not anymore," Andrew said as he rolled his eyes. "Why are you out of the hospital, Mr. Dunbar? I know they didn't just let you walk out into the street still wearing your robe."

"She saved me," Davis said, pointing to Kelly.

"Saved you from what?" Hunter asked.

"That's what I'm trying to tell you. The beast wasn't what we thought. He's a skinny man in a grey suit who kills people. I don't know if he's killing everyone, but my odds aren't looking too hot right now, seeing as he offed Connor in the hospital with magic or something." Kelly rambled.

"I wouldn't call it magic, but he lit that guy like a Christmas tree. Maybe threw gas on him or something. I don't know; I was passed out from the morphine drip I was on." Davis patted his side to remind the others that he was still injured.

"Well, excuse me for giving a shit," Kelly said as she paced the floor, biting at her nails.

"Yeah, why would you give a shit, Kelly? Was it because you thought it would put us back in your good graces?" Hunter said. He had an accusing eye on the girl, and he wasn't about to let her out of his sight.

"No, Hunter. I felt bad about what had happened to him. I'm not as horrible as you think I am."

"Is that so? Because we think you might have left something behind at the Whitcomb house the night you murdered them. A little DNA?" Andrew hissed. He had contempt for Kelly, and she could feel it to her core.

"I was only doing what I was told. Anyway, I was way past gone when the deed was done. You know how I feel about that kind of stuff. Hunter, I can't even hear about what goes on in the morgue." It was true;

Kelly rarely ever let Hunter talk about his work. It was one of the things that kept them from dating.

"Well, the DNA from under the nails confirmed a woman in there, and more than likely, she helped with the killing," Andrew said as he began to inch closer to the telephone on the wall.

"That doesn't mean it's mine. As I said, I knew what would happen, but I didn't participate in that, I swear. Let's stick to the topic at hand. What are we going to do about this guy?" Hunter scratched his head.

"Well, for starters, we need to go to the guy who might have more information on this beast."

"Or we can go back to Claire's. I can pull some strings. She might have her books on this matter; I mean, she did have some pretty powerful stuff going on at that apartment." Hunter nodded at Andrew's statement.

"Either way, this carnage has to end." Kelly said, "Because if he finishes what he came here to do, there will be no stopping them."

Willow and Belle were finally home and rested after the jail excursion. Willow knew Father Hall would be pleased to find out they had managed to do what he wanted. With any luck, Darla would have passed by now, and the Beast was walking the street of Finch Hollow.

Belle was much more of a skeptic than her sister. She had only agreed to work for the group to keep her sister in her life. Only a few weeks into this nonsense, they had already brainwashed Willow into believing what they were doing was for the greater good and that the Beast would put things into perspective. Belle didn't think that anyone named the Beast would do much good and honestly couldn't understand why anyone would think otherwise.

"You don't have to sit by the phone like that, Willow. You know if they need you, they will find you." Willow rolled her eyes and sat beside the old house phone on the chair. Their parents had willed this house to both of them, and shortly after that had died tragically in a car accident.

"Look, I don't know what they want us to do next. But my gut is telling me something big is coming." Willow looked over at the hall clock and realized it was already five in the afternoon. She had completely forgotten to eat, and she was sure her sister had also forgotten. She could feel her stomach begin to rumble. Looking over at her sister, she motioned to the kitchen.

"You want to make us something to eat?" Willow mused and watched Belle roll her eyes, but she did get to her feet and make her way into the kitchen.

"You want me to make a couple of sandwiches?" Belle yelled from the other room. Willow opened her mouth to respond but was cut off by a knock on the door. Getting to her feet, she made her way through the room. Looking through the peephole, she saw a tall thin man in a grey suit holding a briefcase. He was straightening his tie and staring straight ahead. Opening the door, Willow leaned against its frame and crossed her arms.

"Can I help you?" Willow asked, and the man looked at the girl from head to toe.

"Are you Belle Caulders?" The man asked. Willow shook her head no and motioned for the man to enter.

"What's all this about?" Willow asked again, and the man walked over to the chair that Willow had just sat on and placed the case onto it.

"My name is Norman Beast, and I'm an auditor. I look over your deeds and let you know if you are worth keeping or if we need to let you go." Willow's eyes widened, and for the first time, Mr. Beast had arrived; someone believed him without question.

"Would you like something to eat or drink?" Willow asked. She was speaking so quickly that she almost fumbled over the words. "We have been waiting for your return. It's a real honor that you would come to see us." Norman didn't say anything in return to the girl but pulled a piece of paper from his case and looked it over.

Belle ventured from the kitchen when she heard the commotion from the other room. She was holding a plate of sandwiches in one hand.

"Who is this?" She asked as she put the plate down on the table by the door.

"Belle, this is Mr. Beast." Norman nodded and continued to look at the paper.

"So, it looks like you're not a true believer Belle. Why on earth would you want to do the things we ask you to if you don't believe you will get anything in return?" Belle looked around the room and fumbled with her fingers for a moment.

"Who told you that I wasn't a true believer? I do this because I want to." Norman let out a little snicker and looked at the girl for the first time since he had arrived.

"No, that's not true, Belle; I think it's because you love your sister and don't want to see her go to jail for real... Or worse. I think it's because you think you can change her mind and get her out of this without a scar or two to show for it. I admire how you easily lie to my face without flinching, but I cannot have someone like you in the fold. Someone who would try to outsmart me, even though I see everything. I can see into your heart. Willow, could I trouble you for a glass of water?" Willow nodded and disappeared into the kitchen.

"Who are you?" Belle asked as she squinted her eyes at the man.

"Why is it so hard for this town to believe me when I say who I am? You all look into the equation, outweighing everything your mind has ever taught you. I chose this skin because I thought it would help me fit in. Possibly it has worked too well." Willow emerged from the kitchen, holding a glass of water. Presenting it to the man, he nodded and took the glass from the girl's trembling hand. "I fear your services will no longer be needed, Belle." With that, he rolled her paper up like a straw and slipped it into the glass. Taking a long sip. At first, the girl felt a tickle in her throat and began to choke.

"You okay, Belle?" Willow asked, but she knew that something was very wrong. Belle began to vomit, but all that was coming out was water. Gallons of water spilled from the girl's mouth and onto the floor at Willow's feet. Willow's eyes widened as she watched her sister fall onto the floor, her stomach swelling as more water filled her inside.

"I may be a beast, but I'm no monster, so that I will put you out of your misery now." Pulling the paper out of the water, Norman threw it in the air, and when it hit the floor, Belle exploded like an overfilled water balloon. Willow was in shock but also wondered about the man's power. Again, Norman pulled a paper from the case and looked it over. "Ah, yes, Willow Caulders. I enjoy the fairer sex, climbing the ladder in such a miraculous way. Looks like you have quite a way with a bone saw. Connor thought he could lie to me about who did the dirty work. You will be greatly rewarded for your loyalty. The paper went up in smoke, and the Beast shut his briefcase, snapping the latches closed. "I can let myself out." He said as he brushed past Willow, but before he left, he put an ice-cold hand against her cheek. "Thank you again for the water; it was quite refreshing."

It took all day, but Matt and Will had finally made it to Chairman Howard's office. He was always busy doing things, but Matt was sure his Godfather would rush him into the office once he heard of the boy's arrival.

'I'm sorry, Matthew, but Mr. Howards is out for the evening. Can I call you a taxi or your father?"

"That's just the thing, Marcie, I don't know where my dad is, and there is some bizarre shit going on in town right now. We want answers, and the only person I thought might be able to tell us something is Eric." The woman looked exhausted, and Matt felt terrible for putting extra pressure on Marcie.

"Look, all I can tell is when the attack happened, Howards put his two best men on the case." Marcie shuffled a few papers and picked up a business card with Andrew Bower's information. "If you want answers, this is the guy you need to find, but with all the insanity going on right now, I'm not sure where you would begin to start looking." Matt and Will looked at each other and back at Marcie, who had already begun to rub her temples.

"What kind of insanity?" Will asked.

"Well, Claire Snead and Connor Biggs were both killed. Unrelated, but still... Someone out there has a real axe to grind with some of these townspeople, and everyone we've spoken to is tight-lipped about it." Looking at the back of the card, Matt noticed an address and phone number.

"Hey Marcie, maybe we will take that taxi after all."

The four of them had arrived at Claire's apartment, with officer Jenkins at the front door. Kelly felt hesitant about getting out of Andrew's car when she saw how much police presence there was at the building, but Hunter convinced her that it was better to stick with them than to bolt. Andrew had loaned Davis some new threads and rebandaged the wound. At this point, they all thought he would be fine without further hospital interference, primarily when they had heard about what Kelly had seen.

Walking to the front door, they all stopped to talk to the officer, who looked like he had been there for a little while. It could have been all the craziness of the last week, or it could have just been the world on the man's shoulders, but Andrew believed officer Jenkins had aged even more since the night before. Drew knew the man needed a win, precisely what he intended to give him.

"We want to thank you for letting us look at the apartment again, Jenkins; I know it wasn't easy for you to do." The man smiled at Andrew and shook the man's hand. His smile was weathered by the events of the last few days, but he couldn't help but have admiration for the man.

"You need to thank Mr. Howards. It took little effort on my part. The man is optimistic for the two of you."

"Well then, a deal is a deal," Hunter said as he grabbed Kelly's hand and pulled her to the front of the crowd. "I sure hope you can do a better job of keeping this one out of trouble than I ever did."

"Hey!" Kelly said as she tried to free her hand from Hunter's grasp but couldn't. She figured it would have done little to help her case since half the police station was across the street. She wouldn't have made it five feet. She also figured that they would have seen her as dangerous, given the nature of the crimes they all thought she was a part of. She might have ended up dead instead of just in jail. Who knows? Maybe father Hall would find a way to get her out. That was, after all, the plan for Connor.

A chill ran down the woman's spine when she remembered what had happened in the hospital. She didn't want to end up like Biggs.

"Look, we ask that you take the credit for the arrest and make sure she's put in solitary. She may have someone out there looking for her." Andrew began as she took Kelly's wrist. Hunter loosened his grip as he heard the sound of the cuffs being placed on the girl.

"The first part has already been taken care of." Officer Jenkins said as he pulled Kelly away from the men. "I told Howards that there had been a tip, and we arrested her on-site. Marcie has been on the phone with the sheriff for the entire day arranging a single cell, and we've expressly said no visitors in case anyone else is involved in the killings."

"Thanks a lot, Hunter!" Kelly hissed. He could see the hurt in her eyes, but he didn't know what else to do. There was no way they could harbor a fugitive, especially someone that may have murdered three people in cold blood.

"Look at it this way, if what you say is true and you weren't there, you will be charged with something way lighter than first-degree murder, and if you're alone in a cell, then the person or persons out to get you can't touch you. It's a win-win." The man smiled as he pushed past the others and walked inside the building. Davis and Andrew weren't too far behind, and within minutes, the crowd of police had driven away to finish their investigation.

The bellhop had been standing at the door. Hunter was the first to realize that the boy wouldn't take his eyes off him.

"What's up with tall, dark, and weird over there?" Hunter asked Davis, who was the last to enter the building.

"I don't know." Davis said hushedly, "it doesn't seem like the kid likes you. Have you been here before?" Hunter didn't want to think about the last time he had entered the building and accidentally killed Claire Snead. Did the bellhop have a close connection to the woman? Was that why Hunter was getting the evil eye from the kid?

In either case, the three climbed the steps to the second floor and let themselves inside the apartment. Everything was almost the same as they had remembered. The cup of tea on the table was still on its side, but the book was gone. Andrew put his hands on his hips and looked down at the floor.

"They must have taken the book to the evidence locker."

"Well, more than likely." Hunter chimed in. "What did you expect?"

"We might as well get to rooting around here," Davis said as he rubbed his side. After Andrew had fixed his side, the pain had decreased quite a bit from that morning. He didn't know what the man had done, but he knew he had a healer's touch and was grateful for that much.

The three of them had searched the entire apartment in a matter of hours and only produced one thing that might have been useful.

"One book? This woman was a fricking witch, or herbalist or something, and the only thing we could find in this apartment was one lousy book?" Hunter had had about as much of this as he could take. He balled his hands into fists and took comfort in the pain his wounds had created because it took his mind off the failure his life was becoming. "We need a lead; we do, Drew."

"I know what you mean," Drew began as he looked over the black leather-bound book. "I don't think this is the lead we are looking for, though."

"Why do you say that?" Davis asked as he began to rub his side. All the bending and lifting had put a bit of strain on the stitches, and to be honest, the man was worried that much more could make his wound open again. That was something he couldn't afford. All he wanted to do was go home and see his son. No one had told him how he was doing since the attack, and he just knew that if Matthew had come to see him in the hospital today and found him missing, he would freak out.

"All roads lead to the scarlet book. You know, the one that's in Finch Hollow evidence. Probably marked for review and labeled exhibit A." Hunter ran a hand through his hair and let out an exasperated huff.

"Well then, what do you suppose we do then?"

"I don't know how to explain it. It comes in waves Will. All I know is that I fall asleep not knowing something, and I wake up the next morning knowing a little bit more than I did the night before. It's beginning to happen during the daytime too." Will looked over at Matt. They had been driving in the back seat of the taxi for about twenty minutes, and that entire time Matt had been trying to convince Will why exactly they were going where they were going.

"What do you mean, Matt? Are you sure you didn't hit your head or something when you got knocked out at Claire's? I mean, I don't know; I was already unconscious." Matt rolled his eyes and let out a moan.

"No, Will, listen. At first, I couldn't remember why Claire would have wanted us at her apartment, and then it dawned on me, just like I'm sure it did you... You may not want to admit it, but I bet you have these visions too."

"Matt, what your having is probably a side effect of the drugs she filled us with. We have to go on with our life. Your father is missing, which is a concern, but let the police take care of it. That's what they are here for, isn't it?" Will didn't want to alarm his friend any more than he already was, but the visions were also beginning to get to him. He didn't want to talk about them, at least not with Matt. He would have taken them out of context, which the boy did not want to deal with.

"You can say what you want, Will; I know what I know, and I know that the people we want to see are at the apartments up the road from here. I also know that the man who came to the hospital and killed will do it again if he hasn't already. I also know that the only people that can stop him need me for some reason."

"Matt? Do you want me to believe that? It sounds like a fever dream to me." Will looked out of the window, watching the people walking up and down the sidewalk, going in and out of little mom-and-pop shops, kids enjoying their evening, and here he was, in the back of a taxi that smelled of horrible Chinese food and regret. Why was he here? He should be at the hospital, taking all the necessary steps to ensure he was one hundred percent before venturing into the world. Why? Why couldn't he be joyously oblivious like the people on the other side of the street? Why couldn't he be just another teenage boy getting ready for prom? He knew why: Claire had taken what was left of his childhood away with the tea. He also knew that the visions he had been having, mostly in his sleep, were true. He didn't want to know it, but here he was, burdened with the knowledge that something was very wrong with Hannah.

"What have you seen, Will? You must tell me, if not me, one of the men we will meet. I feel like my father is close as well." Matt's eyes widened as they approached the giant Apartment complex. "Wow, how have I lived this close to something so awesome my whole life and never set my eyes on it?" Will turned to look at the building and admitted it was pretty impressive.

"We are here, boys. I assume you want me to put your fare on chairperson Howard's account." Matt smiled as he opened the door.

"Yes, thank you." They were getting ready to get out of the car when the driver asked

"Would you like me to keep the meter running?" Matt smiled as he shook his head.

"No, we can get another ride from here but thank you."

The two quickly crossed the street and walked up to the door. Will grabbed the handle, but the thing wouldn't move.

"Shit, how do you even know that anyone is here?" Will asked as he covered his face with his hands in exasperation. Reaching over to the doorbell, Matt pushed the buzzer. It only took a second before he heard the voice on the other side of the intercom.

"Hello?" The voice said, and for a second, Matt was speechless.

"Dad?" Matt responded. The boys looked at each other as they heard the buzzer unlock the door, and they entered in a rush.

"How did you find us?" Davis asked as he let the boys into the apartment.

"It's a long story, and I doubt you would believe me," Matt said as he walked over to Andrew and held out his good hand. "I want to thank you formally for finding us when you did. I didn't understand why Claire would have wanted to do what she did when I first woke, but now many things are coming to me." Andrew shook the boy's hand and then rubbed the side of his head like he always did when he reached an impasse on a case.

"I wish I could say you had caught us at a better time, but I fear that we may have hit a roadblock in this investigation. I'm starting to fear the worst."

"Hey, aren't you both supposed to be at the hospital?" Hunter asked, putting the black leather book on the table by the old chair Claire always sat in. Even though Hunter hadn't known the woman, it gave him a sense of sadness. He wasn't sure if it was because of her loss or that she had died at his hands. Maybe he hadn't entirely processed the whole thing yet.

"That's another weird story. You may have an easier time believing this one, though." William said with a snort. His eyes were darting around the room, almost as if he thought the old woman was still lurking about, ready to pounce on him again.

"I would tell you to go back there and make sure you were okay, but I think we should avoid the hospital until we find this Norman guy. Seems he likes to set people on fire." Davis muttered.

"Told you..." Matt said, scowling at Will, who just shrugged his shoulders. Matt noticed that his friend was having difficulty taking more than a few steps inside the apartment. Maybe Will hadn't been able to shake off the trauma of being thrown in a locked room for two days as Matt had. Matt had been able to overcome every trauma he had crossed paths with. He was a lot stronger than he had ever given himself credit for.

"We need to start thinking about exploring other places for the answers. We need to get rid of this guy.

There isn't anything here." Hunter said as he walked over to the apartment door.

"Not true!" Matt said as he ran to Claire's room. The others followed to watch the boy rummage through her old jewelry box. "I had a vision on the way over here of this big green gemstone on a gold chain. It's ugly. I don't ever remember Ms. Snead wearing it before."

"Again, with this vision talk," William muttered. "Can't we get the hell out of this death trap? I hate it here."

"What is it supposed to do?" Hunter asked. It was almost as if he believed everything Matt was saying, which confused William. Why? Why would this man, who barely knew these kids think that one... or both of them were seeing visions? Will couldn't wrap his mind around his illusions. What if they were both going insane?

"Ah!" Matt said as he held up the giant green crystal, and just like he had said, it was large and ugly. Something you would see around the neck of a seventies pimp. "I don't know what it does yet, but I'm sure it will come to me."

Kelly heard the electric doors open and then shut at the end of the hallway. Like they had promised her, she was sitting in a solitary cell in an empty room. She could hear the dripping of her sink. It was her only companionship until all of this was over. She hoped that it wouldn't take too long. Finding herself on the wrong end of the sword, so to speak, surprised and frightened the girl.

She could hear footsteps approaching her cell. She had cause for concern, and it was warranted.

"Hello, Kelly." The familiar voice echoed off the walls and inside her head for far too long.

"Beast..." She whispered as he walked into the light dangling from the ceiling.

"Correct." Norman sat on the folding chair that had been placed across from the cell and put his briefcase on his lap, opening the latches and pulling out a paper that was inside.

"No one is supposed to be here. How did you get in here?" The Beast let out a laugh and then grew dreadfully quiet.

"Oh dear, every person has the right to an attorney, and all I had to say was that I represented you in the Whitcomb case. Quite simple, honestly. Now let's get down to brass tax, shall we?" Looking over the paper, Norman smiled and shook his head. "I'm quite impressed by your ability to steal, your rather good at seduction, I see as well; no wonder Connor liked you so much. It's just that I cannot stand a coward and that you have in spades. No, that will not do."

"Wait, wait!" Kelly said, running to the jail bars and grabbing them with her hands so tightly that her knuckles were turning white. "I can change; I'm sure you want something else from me." Norman thought momentarily, putting a slender hand under his perfectly shaved chin.

"No, I can't think of anything I could want from you." With that, the man pulled an eraser from his case and began to erase the words from the paper. At first, it felt like warmth from under her skin, and then it started to burn. Looking down at her skin, Kelly watched in horror as her flesh began to lift and pop from the flesh. Screaming in horror and pain, the woman fell to the concrete floor.

"Stop, please." She said as she watched her body begin to melt. She could hear the sizzling as the white meat began to cook itself from the inside out. She could feel it all, her kidneys bursting and her organs shutting down. She was so warm that the rubber soles of her shoes had begun to bubble and melt.

"I'm a beast, ma'am, but I am no monster so I will let you out of your misery now." Crumpling the paper and putting it back into the case, Kelly took her last breath as she completely melted into a pool of acid, which had begun to eat through the floor of her cell. Getting up to leave, Norman Beast couldn't help but take a good long look at his masterpiece. Some days it was good to be the Beast.

Hannah knew she had to leave the house but didn't know what to do. Mark was intelligent and harbored some magical abilities. At first, she thought about calling Hunter, trying to get them to come over and whisk her away in the dead of night, but then thought better of it. What if they got caught? No, she couldn't risk getting her friends killed, but she wasn't going to sit around and wait for this innocent nonsense to roll in. She was a fighter and wouldn't go down without a fight.

The police had come and gone, and another evening had rolled in. Hannah felt like she was in a horror movie. How was this her life now? After being confident that Mark had gone into his study to smoke,

Hannah made her way to the dresser and put on two layers of clothes. She knew that if she could make it to the bottom of the mountain, someone would let her call her friends. Tiptoeing down the steps, she had almost reached the door when she heard Mark's voice from behind her.

"Where do you think you're going, ma'am? I thought we had an agreement about leaving the house, at least until all of this is over." Turning around to face the man, Hannah let out a heavy sigh.

"The gig is up. I heard everything Mark, how I am the innocent, how you are in cohort with this Beast person." Mark let out a sigh of his own and ran a hand through his thinning hair.

"I believe you may have been mistaken, Hannah. Did you hear me say that you ARE innocent? I highly doubt you did because that's not an accurate statement." Putting a hand on his hip, he reached out to her with the other. "How about we go into the kitchen for some ice cream, and we can talk about this all you want. But honestly, Hannah, I wouldn't make you do anything you wouldn't want to. That's just not how I play the game... And, well, just because the man I work for happens to be not so friendly at times, he is strong and has your best interests at heart." Hannah slapped his hand away.

"I don't want anything from you, Mark. Let me leave if you mean what you say and won't make me do anything I don't want to." A smile ran across Mark's face as he pointed to the door.

"If that's what you truly want, I won't stop you." Hannah's face softened, and she turned to go, but when the door opened, a tall thin man was standing on the other side. Hannah stopped in her tracks. She couldn't take her eyes off him. He was tall and thin and wore a grey suit, holding a briefcase in one hand. He held his hand to the girl, and she eagerly took it.

"Hello, Hannah; I am so sorry to have kept you waiting. I really should have been here before now. It was a shame I missed the death of Zelda Quinn. She was number four on the list in any account." Escorting the girl back inside and shutting the door behind them, Hannah's mood completely changed.

"I can't believe I could have been so wrong about this whole thing. I'm sorry, Mark. Maybe we can have some ice cream and talk about it." Norman smiled at the girl and let go of her hand.

"Why don't you go along and get your ice cream? Mark and I have much to discuss, but we will be along briefly." The girl skipped into the kitchen, and the men looked at each other. "She's better than I could have hoped," Norman said as he put his briefcase on the table and opened the latches. "I can smell the innocence dripping from her; it's disgusting. Do you have Zelda's file with you?" Mark nodded and pointed up to his room.

"Just like you asked." Norman nodded and pulled out the other three, handing them to Mark.

"It's been an absolute pleasure to work with someone as professional as yourself. Just a few more nights, and we can complete our mission." Mark nodded and flipped through the pages of the files he had been given.

"What about the meddling men of Finch Hollow," Mark said.

"I highly doubt they pose a threat, but I've put Father Hall on the case. They should be disposed of this very night."

The five men left the apartment. Andrew locked the door behind them. Matt had put the necklace in his pants pocket for safekeeping. He didn't know why, but he needed to guard the thing with his life. Davis took up the group's rear as they headed down the steps. Davis began to feel eyes on them for the first time that day, and it began to creep the man out.

"Do you have a feeling...." Davis began, but Hunter cut him off.

"Yeah, we are being watched." As the men approached the front door, the bellhop stood in front of it and shook his head no.

"You can't leave here, Mr. Bower." The boy said. Father Hall told us you could never leave here.

"What is that supposed to mean?" Andrew said, but the time for talking had passed because the bellboy jumped on him like a lion on its prey. Flailing his arms wildly at Andrew's face and shoulders. Hunter jumped into action and quickly pulled the boy off of Andrew.

"What the hell is going on here?" William asked as he and Matt pushed the bellhop behind the front counter and tied the kid down with his shoestrings.

"I don't know, but we have some company," Davis said as he pointed at the mob of apartment dwellers finally emerging from their prospective homes. "How many apartments are there in here?" Davis asked as he took a step back.

"Like ten, I think." William began, "Let's get the hell out of here!" Emerging from the back of the counter, the kids could hear the bellhop yelling at the top of their lungs.

"You're a nonbeliever! Father Hall has spoken of you many times at mass. You are an abomination, and you must be destroyed!" Almost like the whole apartment complex was more like an ant colony, the group of people descending the steps all said in unison, "DESTROY!" Turning to escape this nightmare, the five of them were met with a little old lady. She had a baseball bat in her hands. Andrew couldn't believe how fast the lady had to have been to have flanked all five of them, men. Screeching with anger, the woman swung the bat at Andrew's head. Barely dodging the bat's tip, Andrew took a few steps back.

William and Matt had wild eyes and placed themselves back-to-back so no one could sneak up on them, while Davis had taken a more offensive route and snatched the letter opener from the table, hiding the tied-up bell boy.

"You will never get out of here alive, Mr. Bower. Never!" The bellhop began to laugh maniacally. A tall fat man with a mustard-stained work shirt ran at Davis. He didn't have a weapon, but Davis could tell he didn't need one. His fists were as big as mallets and probably just as challenging. Throwing a strong left hook at the man's face, Davis was down for the count.

"Dad!" Matt yelled, which caught the attention of two younger girls, probably the same age as Matt and Will.

"DAD!" They yelled in unison and then giggled. If their lives weren't threatened, Matthew might have even thought they were cute, but not today and not in this building.

The sizeable fat man picked up Davis and shook the unconscious man like a rag doll. Hunter quickly ran to the man's aide, scooped up the letter opener that had been discarded on the floor, and plunged as deep as he could into the fat man's thigh. Screaming in rage and pain, the man let go of Davis and pulled the letter opener from his leg. It didn't take a few seconds before the man was on the floor himself.

"What did you do?" He said, holding his leg with a beefy hand.

"I severed a pretty important tendon. I would go to the hospital as quickly as possible before you have permanent damage. OH yeah, never EVER FUCK with the medical examiner!" Hunter said, smirking, but the smile left his face when he got punched in the face by a shorter old man, the pain was instant, and Hunter's nose began to bleed. "What the..." Hunter was cut off again by the man's little fists.

"I will kill you with my bare hands!" The little man screamed.

"You tell em' honey!" The little old lady yelled back as she swung at Andrew, who was doing his best to dodge her advances. Reaching out with both hands, he managed to grab the bat in the middle. Now it was a tug-of-war competition between the two of them.

The girls had made their way over to Matt and Will, the entire time, they had their hands behind their backs, and the boys knew that couldn't have been a good sign.

"What do you want?" William asked as he lifted his fists by his face. He was ready to fight. He had never hit a girl before, but today looked like a good day to try.

"I will give you a hint," The first girl said. She was average height, with short blond hair. Matt thought he might have had a class with her last year but couldn't remember her name. "It's pretty red and works best outside your body!" The girls put their hands in front of them, the first girl had razor blades between her knuckles, and the second had brass knuckles.

"Shit," Matt said, putting his hands up for the inevitable fight. He couldn't help but look over at his father, who was still motionless beside the fat man, hollering at Hunter.

Hunter had managed to overpower the little man and had tied him up behind the counter in the same fashion as the bellhop.

"We are many, and you are few; we will kill you all!" The bellhop continued to scream.

"Do you ever shut up?" Andrew asked as he finally ripped the bat away from the little old lady and punted her in the face hard enough to knock her out cold. The first girl swung at Will, slashing his arm deeply with the blades. Wasting no time Will hit the girl with an uppercut, knocking her to the floor in front of him. Screaming in rage, she bounced to her feet and bum-rushed the boy. They both fell to the floor, with the girl sitting on the boy's chest, pinning his arms down with her knees.

"Gotcha!" She said with a giggle, kissing him dead on the mouth. "Uh oh, what would Darla say about

our little kiss there? Oh, that's right... She's dead."
Lifting her fist for the fatal blow, William closed his
eyes and waited for death, but it didn't come. Opening
his eyes and looking up again, the girl had a stupid
grin on her face, but both arms were down by her
sides. Slowly, she fell over, freeing William from her
grasp. Warm blood began to pool around the girl's
head. William didn't know what had happened. First,
that is, until he looked over at Andrew, who had a
bloody baseball bat in his hand.

"Thanks," Will said, Andrew, nodded and began to
say something but was tackled by a middle-aged man
in a business suit.

"Die!" He yelled as he tried to wrestle the bat from
Drew's hands.

Matt was left to fend for himself, and the second
girl began to look increasingly insane by the second.
Taking her metal fist, she swung at Matt, who could
barely evade the final blow. Swinging wildly at the
girl, his fist contacted her cheek. Stumbling back, she
regained her balance and ran at Matthew with all her
might. Davis had begun to wake up and noticed what
was going on. Putting eyes on Matthew, he snatched
up the letter opener and went to his son's aide. The
second girl had been swinging at his son's face, and by
God's grace, none of her wild attacks had made
contact, but Davis knew it was only a matter of time
before one of them would.

"Hey!" He shouted at the girl, catching her attention. "Keep your mitts off of my son!" Raging, he ran at the girl and stuck the letter opener in her right eye. Screaming in disbelief, the girl began to claw at her face, throwing the brass knuckles on the floor. Her attempts at pulling the tiny knife out of her face proved to do more harm than good, and she fell to the floor.

Matt and Davis couldn't tell if she was dead or unconscious, but it didn't seem to matter much. She wasn't trying to kill them anymore. Matthew snatched up the knuckles and scanned the room. There weren't that many left, and for the first time, they thought they could get out of this in one piece.

Andrew was on the floor with the businessman on top of him. He had changed his play, and instead of wrestling Andrew for the bat, he was now choking him with it, pushing the wood down hard on the man's throat. Andrew could feel the lights begin to dim and knew he would be out if someone didn't help. Matthew slipped the knuckles onto his right hand and punched the man as hard as he could in the back of the head. Unfortunately, this didn't have its desired effect; the man continued to push down on the bat, almost as if he were utterly unphased by the blood running down his neck. Matthew reached back to swing again, but William grabbed his wrist.

"Need a little help?" He said with a smirk. Matt shrugged.

"Sure, what ya got in mind?" Slipping his arms around the man's shoulders, William put him in a full nelson and lifted him fast and hard, releasing Andrew from his trap. Quickly, he took a deep breath of air. He drank it in and looked at the teenage boy, who was now swinging the businessperson around like he weighed nothing. He was out like a light. Throwing him to the floor, the five walked out of the building together. They could hear the bellhop as they approached the road, screaming, shrill and maniacal,

"YOU WILL DIE, MR. BOWER, YOU HAVE MY WORD!" The laughter faded into the void of the street as they approached the yellow beater and drove off into the night.

Willow knew what she had to do even though she didn't like it. After the beast had left her house, and she was cleaning up what was left of her sister on the floor, she had her first vision. A gift, she supposed, from the beast. Knowledge was a form of power, but not quite the kind she had thought he would give her.

She saw the fight at the hotel and the green gem necklace in Matt's pocket, and she knew that they had escaped from the hotel without being too worse for wear. She also knew they had decided to stay at a hotel right outside of town and that they were in rooms 233 and 234 on the hotel's second floor. She also knew that Hunter had patched up Will's arm, and he was almost as good as new. It was smart not to go home, especially with a bounty on their heads.

Pulling up to the hotel, Willow got out of her rental car, courtesy of Father Hall, who, after hearing what she had to say, was quite eager to help. He seemed like he had something of his own in the works. Willow knew better than to ask too many questions. You don't want to know too much in this line of work, or you might get axed yourself; that was the last thing she wanted. There was a way she could even bring back her sister as long as she did exactly as she was told, but she wasn't interested in that. She was more interested in being on the right side of Norman's army. It would prevail; they were many, and the many always out weight the few.

Pulling the pistol from the glove compartment, Willow slipped it under her belt loop and got out of the car. She had tried to be as late as humanly possible, she didn't want to have the hotel manager see, and she knew that he usually watched the late-night shows with his wife in room one hundred on the bottom floor. That room was reserved for the night Hotel manager, and the phone inside that room was connected to all the other lines in the building.

Slipping around the side of the building, Willow made her way up the fire escape to the second floor. Better to be safe in this case. She had to get to that necklace no matter what the cost. Mr. Beast had told her that it was imperative. Not so much to them but to their ruin. It was always something with these guys.

Why couldn't they give in and let the beast win? There would be no more fear, pain, and power for the chosen. Willow just knew he was her king, and he had all that she wanted.

Matthew woke up with a start and looked over at the bed beside him. His father was snoring lightly, and the sound that used to annoy the boy just a few weeks before now comforted him. He had feared the worst when the large man had knocked his father out. He was already injured from the knife wound. Matt hated that they had been dragged into a new fresh hell almost daily.

Getting to his feet, the boy walked to the bathroom and shut the door before turning on the light. Splashing a bit of water on his face, he looked into the mirror. He almost didn't recognize his face. He looked rattled and war-torn. When was this going to end?

Sitting on the tub's edge, Matt ran his hands through his shoulder-length hair. That is where he sat for what felt like an eternity until he heard a creaking sound in the bedroom where his father slept. Getting to his feet, he walked over to the shut bathroom door. Turning off the light, matt crouched by the door and cracked it open as quietly as he could.

There, pacing around the room, was a girl, probably in her mid-twenties. Matt couldn't see her face, but a whisp of chestnut brown hair fell from underneath the hoodie she was wearing with the hood up. What did she want? Eyes widening, Matt grasped at the pocket of his jeans and relaxed just a little when he realized that the necklace was still tucked safely in his pocket. Something had told him that he would have to keep it close until he knew what it was for.

The girl became agitated when she realized that Matt wasn't in his bed and abandoned her cat burglar to get up, turning on the overhead light in the room and pulling a gun from the front of her pants.

"Alright, Matt, where the fuck are you?" Cocking the gun, she pointed it at his father, who had woken with a start. Pushing the door open with his good hand, Matt stood up and walked out very slowly.

"Who are you?" Matt asked as he raised his hands over his head.

"Doesn't matter," Willow said, scanning the room with her eyes. Matt thought about rushing her, taking her down, maybe even wrestling the gun out of her hands, but it was too sketchy. What if the gun went off and shot his dad? He would never be able to forgive himself if that were to happen. "Where the Hell is that necklace you stole from Claire's apartment?" Matt shook his head no.

"I... I don't know what you're talking about. What necklace?" Willow smirked and aimed the gun at Matt, who, again, grabbed the necklace. "You're not getting it, Ma'am. As I said, I don't know who you are and why you're in my room." Willow opened her mouth to talk but stumbled back. Grabbing the side of her head with her unoccupied hand, she pointed the gun at Matt's father again. Letting go of the necklace, Matt raised his hand in the air once again.

"Last chance," Willow muttered. The sound inside of her head began to leave again. It almost sounded like someone screaming, like someone who was in pain or insane. The screams were unbearable. "How did you do that? Put those screams in my head?" She spoke. Matt could tell that something wasn't right with the girl. He didn't think that she had become as weird and wild as the hotel bunch, but there was something he couldn't put his finger on. Looking down at his pocket, the boy shook his head again.

"Don't hurt my dad." He said, taking a step towards the girl.

"I won't touch him if you give me the necklace. That's all I'm asking."

"Don't do it, son. This is too important. I still don't know what's happening, but you and that necklace must be a big part of the solution."

"I... I can't." Matt said, taking another step closer to the woman, but she didn't waste any more time. Pulling the trigger, she shot Davis in the head directly and then turned the gun on Matt.

"DAD!" Matt screamed as he ran towards the bed. Again, the screaming filled her head like a bullhorn.

"Stop, stop, STOP!" Willow yelled as she put, now both hands against her temples. Backing against the closed bedroom door, Willow felt the veins in her head begin to throb, yet the screaming only got louder.

Matt didn't notice anything other than his father's dead body lying in warm blood. Overcome with grief, the boy began to sob, holding Davis's hand. Willow had fallen to the floor. Her eyes felt like sandpaper as the screaming continued.

"That feeling inside your head, the one you call screaming." Matt began, it's all the pain and anguish you've caused others, and there is no way to get rid of it." Getting to his feet, Willow looked over at the boy. His sadness had been overshadowed by pure rage. "There's nothing you can do now, nothing you can do." Willow didn't know why she felt a wave of depression hit her like a truck, but she had to do something to stop the pain.

Grasping for the door, she desperately searched for the handle. Once she opened the door, she rolled onto the walkway and jumped from the balcony. Sprinting across the room, Matt ran outside and looked into the parking lot. Screeching off into the night, he could barely make out a small black car descending in the opposite direction than the sounds of the sirens approaching the building. His father had given his life to help stop this pure evil, and Matt would stop at nothing to put the Beast to bed.

Officer Jenkins and a few other officers arrived within minutes of the shooting, but Matt gave Will the necklace and sent the three men off alone before the police arrived.

"I know what you have to do with this now." Matt explained, "I'm sure if you have it long enough, you will too." William nodded, and they all left silently to the yellow beater and drove off into the night. Hunter was worried about Matt being there alone when the police arrived, but he knew in his heart that it was the only logical thing to do. There wasn't a lot of time to waste.

Will held the necklace in his hand and stared at it for a long moment.

201

"I got nothing." He said, sighing and lying it in his lap.

"Maybe it will come to you if you don't try so hard," Andrew suggested as they drove on the winding back road that led out of town. Again, Will looked down at the necklace and picked it up, slipping the gold chain around his neck.

"Hey, Will, don't beat yourself...." Hunter's voice trailed off as he saw the boy fall limp for a moment and then sit up with a start. His eyes had turned all white, and he had a blank expression.

"Is everything alright back there?" Andrew asked as he kept his eye on the road. He knew there were people still out there to get them, and they wouldn't even stop at leaping onto the car, which meant they had to be close to figuring out how to stop this.

"Will?" Hunter asked as he put a hand on the boy's shoulder. That did the trick, and he snapped out of his trance. Looking over desperately at Hunter, a smile crossed his face.

"It came to me; I know what we have to do. Keep driving." William said, pointing in the right direction. "There's a door in that field up ahead." He said William was no longer afraid of the visions and had renewed faith that they were relevant.

"What's behind the door?" Hunter asked.

"A moon child, she's the first of the three things we need to defeat the beast, and Matt was right all along. We couldn't have gotten to her at all, even if we did know about the door because we need this to open it." William ran a hand over the crystal. Without Matt and Davis, it would be hard not to finish this thing. It almost didn't feel right, but William would see this thing to the end no matter what.

Norman and Mark had waited for the girl to eat her fill of ice cream and let her fall asleep before they began their ritual. The other two had slipped in as Mark had ushered Hannah back up the steps. Since the Beast's arrival, she had become quite aggregable, and Mark found it quite an improvement over her questionable ways.

"Okay, what is it that we have to do?" Father Hall asked; he kept his distance from the Beast; he knew of the monster's power and didn't want to anger him.

"It's quite simple. The four souls I took from here will represent the four waves of darkness; some people like to call them other things, but we will not go into semantics, will we?" Father Hall shook his head no and looked over at Willow, who had been silent the whole evening. She knew she hadn't succeeded in her mission, and part of her feared that Norman would punish her for it. The screaming she had heard before was still there, but not nearly as loud. How did that boy do it? How did he make her go insane like that? She had him dead to rights, and she just bailed. A ruthless killer made her ass, and she felt weak; that was the last thing she wanted to feel right now. Norman turned his attention to the girl, who couldn't make eye contact with him. She didn't know what to say to him that would make her failure any better.

"Don't be so hard on yourself, you may not have gotten the stone, but you caused unmeasurable sorrow on one of the two children, and they are the most powerful. The one who had the crystal is detained as we speak and may not be of any bother to us; in my eyes, you took out almost half of those meddling men, and that should be celebrated." Norman smiled and took her hand. She finally felt brave enough to look up at the man.

"Yes, but they did something to me, that one kid. I can still hear the screaming." Willow put a hand on her temple.

"That might become useful to me. Surely it will pass with time." Letting go of her hand, the Beast walked to his case sitting on the table. Mark had a file in one hand, and Norman pulled out the other three. Handing one to Father Hall and the other to Willow, they looked down at the folders with mild interest. "Inside these folders is a soul, Father Hall. I gave you Connor; he was the strongest, which will seal your strength. Willow, I gave you Kelly, she was the slickest, and that will give you your visions. Mark, you have Zelda, she's the most ruthless, and that will lock in your telekinetic powers, and of course, I have Kevin."

"What does that do for you?" Mark asked as he lit his pipe and took a puff.

"He was Father Hall's sidekick and probably the most trainable, I will use his essence to control Hannah, and with the fifth soul, the innocent she will be complete."

"I thought you only needed four souls to raise the darkness," Willow said; she couldn't understand why he had to kill her sister. Not that she cared, of course; she was a sociopath who enjoyed lying and killing, but curiosity got the better.

"Technically, yes, but two innocents are much more satisfying, making Hannah unstoppable. She will destroy anyone and anything that dares cross us. We all will take what we want and rule this whole land." The four of them made their way up the steps. The only one who knew what would happen next was the Beast, who was at the edge of his mission. The men might be too late. He would devour the sun and release the plagues, and these poor souls blindly followed the simple promise of power.

"All I'm saying is, why are you and your friends always at the forefront of something like this? Your body count is rising, Matt. I know you are the chairperson's Godson, and now that your father has passed, I am sorry for your loss. By the way, Chairperson Howards would become your legal guardian." Matthew hadn't had time to wrap his head around the fact that Chairperson Howards would be his guardian, Hell, he hadn't even come to terms with his father dying in front of him. His head was reeling, and there for a moment, he thought he might throw up.

"What exactly are you trying to say to me, Officer... What is your name?"

"That's officer Finley, and he's always had it out for Mr. Bower, don't pay him any mind." Officer Jenkins said as he pushed officer Finley to the side. With a scowl, the man wandered inside the crime scene to help with evidence.

"So, let me get this straight. There's a cult in Finch Hollow, and you, your father, William, Hunter, and Andrew have been running from them and trying to stop the end of the world? Did I hear that correctly?" Officer Jenkins scratched his head and then looked down at his notepad. "Is that why Claire Snead abducted you and William? Was she involved?"

"Well, yes and no, but that doesn't matter anymore."

"And the incident at the apartment complex, how can you explain that?" Matt opened his mouth to speak and then shut it again. He knew that the following words out of his mouth might get him arrested. He had visions and knew what happened to unwanted people in the Finch Hollow Prison. "Did you know that quite a few people were assaulted today? One young lady lost her life, and another is in a coma. You wouldn't know anything about that, would you." Matt looked down at the ground and shrugged his shoulders. "Look, kid, normally, under these circumstances, we would give you time to get your affairs in order before jumping right in and questioning you, but to be fair, your kind of talking crazy, and Finley is right about one thing your body count is rising."

"Look, it was all self-defense; these people were trying to kill us," Matt said; he looked up at Officer Jenkins with pleading eyes. Jenkins couldn't tell if he was being played or not. He would have backed Andrew up one hundred percent just a few hours before, but things were getting out of control. He had to stop the madness before the whole town became chaos: cult or no cult.

"Fair enough, but you must tell me which one killed that girl. Someone has to pay for that, and you will all be charged for assault." Pulling out his cuffs, officer Jenkins turned the boy around.

"I wouldn't do that if I were you; that is not unless you want media frenzy on your hands." Jenkins knew precisely who was standing behind him and put the cuffs back onto his belt.

"Chairman, with all due respect, you're not above the law, and your God son broke it."

"How so, Jenkins?" Howards said, putting a hand on his hip. He wore an unwrinkled black pinstripe suit with a matching tie. To Matt, the man always looked more like a model than a politician. "Didn't you hear the boy? It was self-defense, and if you want to pursue this matter further, you will go through our lawyers. You're releasing this boy into my custody, and you will do so right now. He's grieving the loss of his father and needs to be home with his family." With a deep sigh, officer Jenkins knew that the man was right, and even if he weren't, Howards could make the whole police station hell on earth to work for if he didn't do what he was told.

Taking the boy by the elbow, the two began to walk down the steps and into the parking lot.

"What have you gotten yourself into this time, Matt?" Howards asked, letting go of the boy's arm. Matt heard the words but couldn't hear the anger in the man's voice that he thought would have indeed been there.

"I will explain everything, but we have work to do," Matt exclaimed as they made their way to the sleek, black car that a security guard was staffing.

"What do you mean?" Howards asked. They both got into the back seat and were driven back into town.

"I know this is going to sound crazy, but the guys and I stumbled onto something big, like end of days big, and they will need my help. They are going to need our help."

William, Andrew, and Hunter walked into the field. They had parked the car around the corner and down a dark alley so no one could see it from the road. Someone could be there, waiting for them when they return, but that was a risk they would have to take.

"Are you sure we are going the right way?" Hunter asked as the three of them continued towards the mountainside.

"Yes, I'm sure of it," William responded excitedly. The closer they got to the door, it would seem, the more pumped William had become.

"I don't like how close we are getting to the mountain. That's the only thing separating us from

Coral Bay, and that place gives me the creeps." Hunter muttered under his breath.

"You don't believe all that nonsense, do you, Hunter? Some of it was beyond ridiculous." Andrew rolled his eyes and pushed some high brush out of his way.

"I didn't until this week happened, and I feel like I'm living in a crazy town." There was a faint glow on the horizon, and the three knew it was the door. Pointing straight ahead, William sprinted off ahead of them.

"There it is!" He shouted. Hunter and Andrew had a bit of a time keeping up but kept the boy in their sights. William walked up to the door and stopped, taking in what he saw. At the base of the mountain, no less. No wonder no one had seen it before because no one in this town would stumble out here for any reason. It was far too close to the cursed city, which might rub off on perfect little Finch Hollow.

William looked at the plain, tan wooden frame and the brass handle and wondered if it could be true. There was no way to know until he tried. Slipping the necklace off and freeing the crystal from its chain, William slid it into a divot at the top of the door. Anyone with eyes could see that it was made for the amulet. First, there was a rumble; at first, Andrew thought it was a rather heavy truck or something driving past, but the second rumble proved that it wasn't the case. Hunter's eyes widened as the doorknob began to turn, and the door swung open. Inside was nothing, darkness and cold deafening silence. It gave Hunter the creeps. He took a step back, but William, on the other hand, stepped as close as he could to the open door. His toes touched the threshold.

"I wouldn't do that if I were you," Andrew advised walking over to the boy, but he hadn't heard a single thing that Andrew had said. It was almost like the boy was in a trance, and there was no snapping him out of it. Thrusting his right hand through the blackness, Hunter and Andrew waited nervously for something to happen.

"Where are you?" William whispered. "We need you back... Where are you?" Suddenly, another hand grabbed William by his wrist, reaching back through the door. "Help me!" The boy yelled as he began to pull the person through the inky void. "We have to save her." Andrew and Hunter ran to his side and grabbed him by the arms. With all three of them pulling, they managed to free the girl from prison. As soon as she was through the door, there was another rumble, and it shut behind them. The amulet fell to the ground with a little thud, and Andrew quickly picked it up.

The force of reentry had the girl lying on top of William, but he didn't seem to mind.

"I never thought I would see you again." He exclaimed as he wrapped his arms around her tightly.

"I was lost in there, it felt like a lifetime, but then I heard your voice Will; I heard your voice." Lying her head on his chest for a moment, the two almost forgot where they were, and all was right with the world.

"How, how are you here?" Hunter stammered as he took a step toward the love birds. Darla and William got to their feet, and William slipped his hand into hers.

"I got the stone," Andrew said as he walked towards the three of them. It was the first time he had seen who had come through the door, and it made him stop in his tracks and go a little slack-jawed.

"Darla?" The girl was completely healed, exactly like they had remembered. Her mahogany brown hair shimmered in the moonlight, and her almond-shaped eyes and mocha skin were flawless. But how?

"I remember everything, Andrew; I didn't fall from the tower. That Tuesday, I was murdered, just like the others; only mine wasn't because of magic."

"What do you mean?" Andrew asked; he still had the amulet in his hand, and he could feel it getting warm, almost as if the moon was charging it.

"Mark, he has these powers; he's the one who's in charge. He can make people do things. Even kill themselves. Father Hall has them now too, but he has this weird way of making people believe what he says; he's also strong."

215

"Who killed you? We have to know, was it Father Hall?" Will asked as he tightened his grip on Darla's hand.

"No, you see, I was going to jump from the tower, but my mother got into my head and coached me down. Father Hall was there, but he never left the building. As I was heading out onto the street, a girl, Willow, hit me with a car, and for good measure, she got out and hit me in the back of the head with a mallet to make sure it looked like I jumped."

"I knew something wasn't right. I felt it from the jump." Hunter muttered. "How do we stop them?" William took the amulet from Andrew and slipped it back onto its chain. Handing it to Darla, she put it on her neck.

"I believe this belongs to you." Darla nodded, and the three noticed that the crystal had begun to glow. It wasn't nearly as ugly in the moonlight.

"You have completed the first task by freeing the moon child. I have a present for you, but I cannot give it to you until it's time."

"What is it?" Hunter asked.

"The beast's real name. Know its name, and you have power over him. It weakens him, but you can only use it once...." William answered.

"You said there were three things; what's the last thing we need?" Andrew asked as they all began to walk back to the car.

"My body, my moon dust."

Jenkins and Finley decided to keep an eye on Matt and Eric for the time being. Something didn't add up in this town, and the two officers thought that Matt directly had something to do with it.

"You don't think the boy killed his father, do you?" Finley asked as he took a sip of coffee. Jenkins looked out the car window, and up at the significant estate the chairperson lived in. He guessed that Matt would live there, too, now that Davis had passed on.

"No, I don't think he did, but I think he knows who did, and he's keeping it from us."

"Why would he do that?" Finley asked as he matched glances with Jenkins.

"That's just the thing; if your father was murdered in cold blood and you knew who it was, wouldn't you want justice?" Finley nodded and took another sip of coffee.

"You think he's going to go after them himself?"

"Yea, yea, I do... And they are going to make a move tonight. We are going to lay low and follow them. This ends tonight."

Matt paced the room as he explained what was happening all over town to his God Father. Eric listened carefully to what the boy had to say without interrupting.

"It's starting to go away now, but I had visions about what would happen and how to fix it. I know William has had them too. I think Claire gave them to us as a fail-safe. To help us stop the Beast."

"Well then, what's the next course of action, son? If everything you're telling me is true, then we don't have much time to sit around and twiddle our thumbs." Matt nodded and stopped pacing; turning over to Eric, he pointed to the phone that began to ring moments later.

"That's what we have to do. It's going to sound crazy, but the guys need us." Picking up the phone, he had a quiet conversation with the person on the other end of the line and then hung up the phone quietly. "Well?" Matt asked as he stared at the chairperson.

"I guess you're going to Finch Hollow Crematorium, and you'll pick up Darla Snead's ashes." Howards ran a hand over his face in exasperation; he felt like this was some twisted game. He had no reason not to believe his God Son, though; he needed answers to know what happened to Davis.

"Let's do this!" Matt exclaimed as he ran to the door, but Eric stopped the boy.

"I can't go with you; if this got out and I were somehow involved, I would surely lose the next election. But you can take the car and Agent Keen." There wasn't time to argue with his God Father, and he knew it would have done him little good to do so anyway. Snatching the keys off the counter and finding Agent Keen at the front door, the two ventured out into the night, neither knowing that the officers were waiting in the shadows to flank their every move.

Driving across town to the crematorium, they both got out of the car just in time to see a little old man greeting them at the front door with a set of keys in one hand. He seemed friendly enough, but Matt had been fooled before.

"Keen," Matt whispered, "Make sure you keep one hand on that gun. We can't trust anyone in this town." Keen nodded and unstrapped his piece. Walking to the front door, the little old man smiled and waved them inside.

"Eric called while you were on the way down. Said something about picking up ashes for a family member?" The little old man walked over to the wall and snapped the light switches on, leaving the three of them in a blinding light. It didn't help that the walls and furniture in the place were also white. It was hard to see what was right in front of you.

"Who are you?" Matt asked as he followed the man down the hall.

"I'm George, the replacement funeral director. Originally from Eagles Nest."

"What happened to the old Funeral Director?" Matt asked, becoming increasingly concerned.

"Didn't you hear? News usually goes fast around here, well, in all little towns, I would assume. He retired a few weeks ago. Went to Boca Raton, I think." Walking up to a big white door with the words Employees Only on the front in bold red, George pulled out a set of keys and began to rummage around, looking for the right one. "I wouldn't have guessed anyone would be out here this time of night, especially to pick up an urn. It ain't going anywhere, ya know. Ah, here's the key." Slipping the key into the lock, the little old man opened the door with a little creak.

Keen was the first person to hear the noise from the back of the room. The shelves of urns and boxes made it virtually impossible for them to see what was causing the noise, but Keen wasn't taking any

221

chances, pulling the gun from his holster and pointing it in front of him.

"Get behind me, you two." They did as they were told, and the three of them made their way through the maze of shelves.

"Where are we going?" Matt asked as they began their walk.

"Fourth aisle, third shelf to the right, S and T." The three heard shuffling getting closer, but they had no way of knowing where it was coming from. The shelves played games with the noises surrounding them, echoing off the walls and making them seem to come from all around them.

"If you're in here, now would be the time to let us know, I am armed, and I will shoot," Keen yelled. The shuffling sound stopped, and a voice behind them made them all turn around. The old Funeral Director was standing there with Darla's ashes in his hands. They had chosen a tasteful silver urn with the name Snead engraved on the front.

"Looking for this?" The man said with a snort.

"I thought you had retired," George said as he made his way to the front of the group.

"I did, but I thought I would make one last visit; I needed to do one more favor for an old friend."

"Well, thank you for finding the urn, but we were more than capable," George took a step forward, but the man took a step back, pulling a small pistol out of his belt loop and pointing it at the little old man's head.

"Hold it right there! You three aren't going to get these ashes! Not tonight!" Keen pushed past the other two and pointed his weapon at the director.

"I suggest you hand the urn over now, and no one gets hurt." Letting out a laugh, the director cocked his gun, and that was all Keen needed, firing off a round into the old man's head and snatching the urn from his wavering fingers before it could hit the floor.

"Oh, oh my!" George said as Keen ushered them out of the room, but they had barely reached the front door before Jenkins and Finley burst through the crematorium doors, guns in hand.

"This is the Finch Hollow Police! You are under arrest." Jenkins said but was stopped in his tracks when he met with Keen.

"I am special Agent Keen with the Finch Hollow Secret service, and the man you want is in the back with the dead. He attacked us with a gun unprovoked, and I was protecting them, which I was sworn to do." The two officers had no choice but to holster their weapons and stand down. What else was going to go wrong for them tonight? They were thwarted at every turn.

"What were you three doing here this late at night anyway?" Finley asked as he put a suspecting hand on his hip.

"You wouldn't believe us if we told you." Matt began.

"Speak for yourself. I got a call to come into work." George exclaimed as he put his hands up in the air.

"Put your hands down." Keen said, "You're not in trouble."

"Well, spill it," Jenkins said, taking Finley's side and putting a hand on his hip. He needed to know what was going on. He needed to put a stop to the violence.

"I think it may be easier just to show the two of you," Matt said, "but you will have to trust us. You will get the answers you're looking for and put away some pretty nasty people. If everything goes as planned, the violence and chaos will stop tonight."

"AAAAAAA!" Willow screamed as she paced the third floor of the cabin. The others had wandered downstairs after the ceremony, and Hannah hadn't woken up yet. Willow offered to take the first watch and let them know once she had risen. So far, everything was going according to plan everything, that is except for Willow's power. The screaming inside her head was getting louder, and she knew it was muffling the visions. She couldn't tell the men that she knew where the meddling men were. That would put her on Norman's shit list. She was surprised that he hadn't punished her earlier.

Downstairs the men had retired to the parlor. Mark was smoking his pipe, Norman was going over papers in his briefcase, and Father Hall was pacing the floor, ready in wait for what was to come.

"Are you sure they are coming?" Hall asked as he glanced out of the window.

"You can bank on it. I felt the door open, which means one of those visions having children extracted the moon child." Norman took a deep breath and continued to look through the folder he had in his hands.

"That's not good for us, Norman; it's horrible." Mark put down his pipe and crossed his legs, looking over at the priest, who reminded him of a feral cat locked in a cage—pacing the floor, clenching and unclenching his fists.

"You're over thinking things again. I mean, it's been dumb luck that they have gotten this far, and in any case, they are no match for any of us." Father Hall nodded but refused to stop pacing the floor.

Matt and Keen drove to the mountain's base, where they saw the yellow beater parked in the darkness. Matt might not have noticed it if it weren't for the vibrant color.

"Stop," he told Keen, and the agent pulled to a halt, parking right behind the beater. The two of them got out of the car and walked over to the yellow car. Touching the hood, Keen nodded and pointed up the mountain.

"It's a bit of a walk, but we can probably catch up to them if we go. The engine is still warm." Matt was holding the urn in his arms like a small child. He knew that he had to keep it safe at all costs. He knew that this was the last piece of the puzzle and that they could all put this monster back in the box it flew out from.

As they began their walk up the mountain, they could hear the faint sound of the police car rolling up to the front of the driveway and parking so no one could come or go by car. Keen requested a walkie and explained what they had to do to the officers.

William, Darla, Hunter, and Andrew had more of a head start than the others had anticipated and were standing in the shadows on the south side of the cabin. Darla and Will had not stopped holding hands the entire time they had been hiking, and Hunter found it endearing to be young and in love.

"Okay, we are here; what do we do now?" Hunter asked, looking over at the couple.

"Well, if these people have the powers you claim they do, we can't just roll in and attack. They probably know we are here by now anyway." Andrew said. He had had about as much of this as he could take. He couldn't stand the idea of any more of his friends dying.

"They have their suspicions but don't know we are here," Darla said as she used her free hand to touch the glowing crystal around her neck.

"How do you know that?" Will asked. He could tell that his visions were starting to dwindle. This both calmed him and made him a bit concerned. He hoped that they stay long enough to see this all through. They had, after all, come in quite handy.

"The crystal imprinted on the one with the visions. I can tell because I can feel her rage and agony. All she can feel right now are the screams of her victims. However, Willow is a ruthless killer who loves what she does." William nodded at the girl and took a few more steps closer to the house, but Andrew raised a warning hand.

"Be careful, you two; Mark has motion lights on this side of the house. We don't want to announce ourselves just yet."

"I say we go after Hannah first, get her outside, and one of us can get her back down the mountain to safety. It's the only direct course of action I can say is the most important right now." Hunter muttered to the others, and they all agreed.

"Getting rid of the Beast is one thing, but banishing the plagues is another matter entirely." Darla began,

"What are the plagues?" Andrew asked, "I feel like you failed to mention any plagues."

"They feed the powers that were given to the people inside of the house, and the beast, well, he feeds on their souls. Eventually, the evil inside of them will consume what little humanity they have left, Hannah included. She will not be the person you remember until we banish what they put inside of her. Oh, and once she awakens, their powers will only get stronger."

"Well then, we strike while the iron is hot." A voice said from behind them. Matt and Keen were coming up the mountain, urn in hand. A goofy smile crossed his face when he set eyes on Darla. "Oh, my God!" He said as he put his free arm around the girl. Darla let out a little giggle, and the three felt content for the first time in a long time, even if it were just fleeting.

"So, what's the game plan?" Keen asked as he unholstered his gun.

"Who is this?" Hunter asked, feeling a little uneasy around the tall, broad-shouldered man with the gun.

"Don't worry, that's Keen. He's Howard's, right-hand man. He helped us get this." Matt held out the urn to Darla, who took it, thanking him with a kiss.

"You're the best." She said and then looked over at William. "You both are."

After a brief conversation, the six of them hashed out a plan. Keen led the charge to the back door, careful not to set off the automatic motion lights in the driveway. Andrew noticed the blood stain as they passed, but Darla didn't seem too upset. Maybe this girl wasn't Darla; Andrew couldn't find any logical reason that it should be. After all, she died in his apartment, and now she was holding the ashes of her former self. He didn't like being left out of the loop, but he supposed that was how things would have to be if they wanted to finish this thing once and for all.

Crouching down by the back door, Keen took out a small lock-picking kit and began whittling away at the doorknob.

"Your guy's efficient," Hunter said as he looked over at Matt.

"It's a standard issue. All of us have one of these, a pistol, and a badge that lets us park wherever we want." With that being said, the door creaked open, and the meddling men entered the cabin's first floor.

They could hear the people over the top of them but couldn't make out what they were saying.

"You know what you are supposed to be doing, so let's split up and squash this thing," Keen said, nodding at the other five. William and Darla made their way up the steps towards the sound of the commotion with Matt and Keen at their six. Andrew and Hunter stayed on the first floor, making their way to the conservatory.

"We have to find out all we can about these plagues." Andrew said, "Darla said we can get rid of the Beast, but that won't stop the plagues inside Hannah."

"We have to save her," Hunter said in agreeance. "She's been through far too much already." Once they were confident that they were alone on the first floor, Andrew pulled a small flashlight out of his coat pocket, and they began to sift through the shelves of books with a sense of urgency.

William and Darla were the first to pass the cracked door. As they passed, they could see the group inside the parlor and smell the pipe Mark had been smoking. They quickly passed by and made their way to the next steps. On the other hand, Matt stopped in his tracks when he saw Willow in the far corner, checking her nails and leaning against the wall like she didn't have a single care in the world. Almost as if the murder she had committed didn't seem to matter. Matt could feel the anger well up inside himself, and he almost couldn't stop himself from barging into the room and killing the girl with his bare hands.

Keen put a hand on the boy's shoulder and shook his head no.

"Wait for it," Keen mouthed, and Matt did as he was told.

"Where are these losers?" Willow asked as she looked over at Mark, who had begun to look over a few papers that Norman had handed him.

"I'm sure they will be here at a suitable time, dear." Father Hall was still pacing the floor with his hands behind his back. At this point, beads of sweat had begun to form on his forehead. He wasn't as confident about how this would play out.

Pulling a small switchblade knife from his back pocket, Keen handed the weapon to Matthew as he pulled his gun from the holster and kicked the door open.

"You're all under arrest," Keen said in a demanding voice, and the three people in the room looked at the two guys and began to laugh.

"What exactly is it you think you're going to do?" Mark said with a snort. Keen pointed the gun at Mark's head and cocked the gun.

"I could very easily shoot you where you sit." Keen retorted as he took a step forward. Mark nodded and lifted his hand.

"You could certainly try." Moving his hand towards his head, Keen could feel himself lose control of his body. Slowly moving the gun to his head.

"What are you doing?!" Keen asked, but Matt knew what was going on, and he knew he had to plan this out perfectly. Keen shut his eyes and waited for the inevitable to happen, but right at the last second, when he felt his finger on the trigger begin to press down, Matt pushed the weapon away from Keen's head. The gunshot sound was loud and lethal, catching Willow in the neck. The girl began to gurgle and claw with her hands at the hole in her throat.

Falling to the floor on her knees, a look of astonishment and fear in her eyes.

"That's right, you bitch. That was for my dad," Matt could feel the tears welling up in his eyes, but he swallowed them down before anyone else could see.

"You idiots, do you think I care about her? She's nothing in the grand scheme of things, and her power will be divided between us later." Mark said without even trying to get up. Again, Keen pointed the gun at Mark, and this time Father Hall took refuge behind the door just in case the same thing happened to him. Again, Mark lifted his hand to his head, and again the agent put the gun to his head, but this time he pulled the trigger; Hall and Randolph both expected to hear the gunshot again, but this time was only met with a click. Matt began to laugh as Mark let go of Keen's body.

"Do you think we would bring a loaded gun here? Nope, not knowing what we know about you." Matt smirked, pointing the finger at Mark. Father Hall stomped out from behind the door in a rage. Letting out a battle cry, he charged Keen, who dropped the gun and put his arms up, ready to fight, but he was no match for Hall. With one decisive blow, the priest walloped the man in the chest, and he flew out of the open door across the hallway and through the adjacent wall.

"Go get the Beast; he has to know they are here." Mark nodded and got out of the chair. Pointing at the boy, he wiggled a finger and pointed at the chair. Matt was no match for Mark's powers and was utterly compelled to sit and stay put. Father Hall made his way out of the room to finish what he had started, and Mark ventured up to the second floor to find Norman, who had been spending the ceremony that would give them ultimate power.

Darla and William had made their way to the last room on the top floor. They could see flickering lights inside and smell strange incense burning.

"She's gotta be in there," William said, nodding to the bedroom door.

"The Beast cannot be too far behind where the plagues are," Darla said, holding the urn with her free hand. Pushing the door open, the two of them entered the room. Hannah was lying there on the bed in a white cotton gown. If William didn't know better, he would have thought that the girl was sleeping, but he was an expert at noticing the tiny mannerisms of a magically induced coma. It would likely make things easier for the Beast to transfer the souls.

"Hannah?" Darla whispered as she took a step closer to the girl. Kneeling by the bedside, the Moon Child took Hannah's hand and pressed it against her chest. "I sure hope the guys will be able to find out how to fix her." William could hear the distress in the voice of his love, which broke his heart.

"I'm afraid your friends will run out of time before they find out how to stop her. It will be a glorious win for me." Turning to face the man, William turned white with fear. Norman no longer looked like a thin, boring old man but a giant, man-eating monster with brown scales and a single horn on the top of his head that branched off into two at the top. His black, shark-like eyes had no pupils, but he could feel them boring holes into their souls. The one thing the beast did have that Norman kept close was the case; he was holding it in one monstrously large, clawed hand. It would have almost looked comical if the kids weren't horrified by the beast.

"I may not be able to stop the plagues... just yet, but I can stop you." Darla hissed as she pushed William behind her.

"That may be true, but that was always going to be the way. I will go back through the door. Eventually, I will find my way home again... I always do." The Beast let out a little snort, and a puff of smoke wafted from his reptilian-like nostrils. "Unlimited power corrupts ultimately."

Opening the urn, Darla threw the ashes at the monster, who fell back into the hallway. Norman covered his eyes and let out a howl of pain, dropping the briefcase beside him. Mark was ascending the stairs just in time to see the Beast begin to get taken down. Scrambling down the hall, he snatched the briefcase and vanished into the next room.

"Nooooo!" Norman backed out as Darla stormed up to the dragon. Pulling the Necklace from around her neck and slipping it over the beast's head, she looked up at the sky with a sense of accomplishment. Putting her left hand on the crystal, still glowing, she looked at the menacing beast.

"I know your name!" She yelled, "I know your name, and when I say it, you will leave us and this town, and you will disappear from our presence." Norman struggled to free himself from the small girl's grasp, but her strength and belief were too muscular for the giant.

"You, you don't have to do this, Moon Child. You can have ultimate power." The beast began, but Darla smiled at the reptile and continued.

Your name is Zaglobac, be away from my sight. Do not return." The monster began to shake, almost like an earthquake inside of him, and then he began to smoke. Keeping her hand on the stone, Darla turned her head towards William.

"I have to go now, my love." She said; William's eyes widened in fear and sadness as Moon Child and the Beast burst into flames.

"Darla, No!" He screamed as he took a few steps forward, but the girl shook her head no.

"It always had to be this way." She said, "Know I will always be with you, inside your heart. Until we meet again, know that I love you."

"I love you too," William said as he fell to his knees. The flames were large and threatening at first, but then, a brilliant ball of green light bottled it up and vanished, almost as if Darla and the Beast had never been there. The only thing left was the green crystal necklace, lying discarded on the hallway floor.

Rolling over onto his side Keen reached for the walkie in his pocket. He could hear Father Hall stomping out of the other room and making his way into what Keen thought could only be described as a storage room. Putting the walkie up to his mouth, he pushed the button.

"Officer down, requesting backup." That was all Keen could say before Hall was standing over him, his fists balled up.

"There is no good outcome for you. I've never seen you before; how did you even get involved with these no-good kids?" Hall wrenched back his right fist, ready to punch Keen in the face, but the man wasn't expecting what came next. Without hesitation, Keen

239

lifted both his legs clocking Father Hall as hard as he could in the balls. Letting out a pain-filled scream Hall fell to the floor beside Keen. Scrambling to his feet, the agent looked down at the priest.

"I have to protect Mr. Dunbar to the best of my abilities, and Father, just because you have power doesn't mean you have the skills to use it." Wandering out of the room through the hole that Keen's body had made moments before, crossing the hall, and walking back into the study, he looked over at Matt, who was still struggling to get up from the chair.

"I take it you stuck there...." Keen said, scratching his head. "I've never seen someone with that sort of power." Matt nodded and looked up at the ceiling.

"He went upstairs, and I could hear the commotion from the chair. Something happened; you have to take a look." Father Hall, recovering from the blow, slowly got to his feet. Enraged by the big man in the suit, he made haste after Keen. He stopped only for a moment when he heard the front door kicked in by Jenkins and Finley. Both of the offers had their guns drawn and began to make their way down the hall to the door they had seen Hall vanish into. Stopping in shock as Matthew, still sitting in the chair, was flung out into the hallway, he landed on his side with a loud bang.

"I'm going to kill you, you giant oaf!" Hall screamed as the three of them in the hallway could hear things being knocked around. The blow from being thrown across the room had knocked the breath out of Matt's chest, but he finally removed himself from the chair.

"What's going on?" Jenkins asked as he inched closer to the door.

"Father Hall is the influencer; he caused the riot in the apartment, and the woman on the floor is the one who shot my dad. If you looked around this place long enough, you would find the murder weapon and gunpowder residue on her fingers." Matt ran down the hall and began to go up the stairs.

"Where do you think you're going?" Finley asked with a smirk.

"I have to help my friends. Something is telling me it will get worse before it gets better."

"I found it!" Hunter said as he jumped to his feet. Andrew walked over and looked at the book Hunter had been reading. "It took me some time to reference the beast and his correlation to the plagues, but I think I know how to stop it."

"Enlighten me, and things are starting to sound sketchy out there," Andrew said as he looked out across the room. He was pretty surprised that no one had followed them into the conservatory; he was even more surprised that when the police ran through the door that they didn't bother coming near them. It must have been pure chaos for them not to have been discovered.

"Here," Hunter said, pointing to a passage in the old text. "The Beast solidifies his earthly realm by harboring four plagues, sealed by an innocent's blood."

"What are the plagues?" Andrew asked as he looked back at the book. He could hear a tussle going on a few rooms over and could only imagine who it could be.

"Looks like Famine, disease. Eternal darkness and something called the rising."

"The rising?" Andrew asked, but all Hunter could do was shrug his shoulders.

"I could go on another man hunt for whatever the rising is, but I think we have bigger fish to fry." Andrew nodded and continued to listen to his friend. "So apparently, to be a sacrifice, you must engage in a contract, like for something you want. If the Beast deems you worthy, you get whatever your heart desires. If not... Boom, sacrifice. We have to find those papers and destroy them. That should stop the plagues... each soul represents one plague."

"If I were a beast, where would I hide my contracts." Andrew said, "I don't know, but we should head upstairs. If anyone would, it's the boys." Hunter nodded and put down the book.

"Let's go." Venturing out into the hallway and up the steps, Drew and Hunter saw the two police officers inching closer and closer to the door; the

243

walls on the other side were bowing and cracking under the weight of the two inside, pummeling each other to death. Finally, Jenkins had had enough and rushed into the room, pointing the gun at Father Hall, who lifted Keen up in the air with one hand. It was almost as if the giant special agent weighed nothing to Hall. Finley walked in behind his partner; his eyes widened when he saw what was happening.

"Sir, I'm going to have to ask you to put officer Keen down now, or I will have to use lethal force." Jenkins pointed the gun at the priest, but the man merely laughed and threw Keen across the room. Hitting his head hard on the table as he came down, the man went limp onto the floor. A pool of blood began to form around his head. Jenkins cocked the gun and continued pointing it at Hall, who was smirking. He didn't look at all concerned.

"You know, at the beginning of all of this, I was worried that I wouldn't be able to hold my own, but after little Willow over there got a bullet to the neck, I felt her energy flow through me like a wave. Hell, I'm even more powerful than I even knew possible."

"That might be so, but I doubt you're more powerful than my pistol," Jenkins said, taking a step closer to Father Hall.

"That may be so, but you don't want to shoot me. You want to shoot your partner over there." Hall pointed to Finley.

"You know something," Jenkins said, "I believe your right." Turning his gun on Finley, he pointed it at the officer's head. Finley cocked his gun, and instead of pointing it at Jenkins, he told it at Hall.

"You don't want to do this," Fin said as he began to take a step closer to Jenkins. He didn't want to die, but if he had to, he would take Father Hall with him.

"Yes, I do," Jenkins said, "He told me to." Pulling the trigger on the gun, Jenkins shot Finley in the chest; taking a staggering step back, Fin's eyes stayed steadfast on Hall, who was grinning ear to ear. That was all Finley needed. Pulling the trigger on his firearm, he shot at Hall, and his aim was true, striking him right between the eyes.

As Hall's body hit the floor, Jenkins dropped his gun and ran to his partner's side.

"Oh my God, I didn't mean to...." Finley put a hand in the air.

"I will be okay." Opening his shirt, Finley exposed his bulletproof vest. "I don't know how you knew."

"I didn't." Hunter and Andrew met up with the officers, and they all made their way up the steps to face their following and last challenge.

"It's almost 3 in the morning," Hunter said as they slowly ascended the steps.

"Is that important?" Andrew asked; he was taking up the rear and kept eyeing the bottom of the stairwell; he didn't want to be taken by surprise.

"I'm not sure, but the book kept referencing the number three."

Reaching the top of the stairs, they could hear the old grandfather clock at the end of the hall striking three, and they could also see Matt standing at the front of one of the rooms. He was holding his hand out and motioning for someone to come out. The group walked towards them, but the two officers stopped at the room right before, drawing their weapons.

"I think there is someone in there," Jenkins said. Finley pressed his ear to the door and nodded.

"He's talking to someone. There might be two."

Drew and Hunter stood behind Matt, looking into the darkly lit room. Matt's hand collapsed on the floor, looking defeated. The green crystal was now around his neck, and Darla was nowhere to be found.

"What happened?" Andrew asked as he gazed into the room.

"Darla banished the beast, but it took her with him," Matt whispered. "I want him away from Hannah; I don't know what she will do when she wakes up." Hunter pushed past the two of them.

"Let's just snatch him up." That was all he said before halting with a start. Hannah sat in bed and looked down at William, who had been crying on the floor.

"Who are you?" Hannah asked, but it wasn't Hannah's voice anymore; it was the sound of four distinct voices within her. Grabbing the boy by the back of the neck, she stood on top of the bed, whisking William into the air.

"We know who you are!" Hunter yelled. They all began to feel the air around them thicken and start to rush around them. It almost felt like a tornado, cold and calculated but most deadly.

"We are the plagues; we will devour your world." Andrew looked over at Matt, who hadn't taken his eyes off William, who had begun to struggle for his freedom.

"We have to find the binding contracts and destroy them," Andrew said. "Do you know where they are?" Matt nodded.

"I'm not having the visions anymore, but the one I did have about the man who killed Connor, he was carrying a briefcase, and William said that the man from downstairs grabbed it when Darla and the Beast were struggling. That's where they are. I guarantee it." Matt pointed to the door that the police were standing at.

Mark hid inside the room for a while, hugging the case against his chest like a football. He had hoped Father Hall would take care of these meddling men, but now he knew that he would have to take matters into his own hands when he heard the clock chime three.

Putting the case under the desk in the corner, Mark walked to the door, but before he could unlock it and open it, he heard a voice from behind him.

"You play an excellent game of wheel of the apocalypse." Turning to face the voice behind him, he saw a young man standing beside the desk.

"Who the hell are you?" Mark asked as he motioned for the man to sit, but he did nothing.

"Yeah, that stuff doesn't work on me. I'm not from around here. Raz and I are here to recruit a few of your kinfolk out there after all this is said and done, one way or another." Pulling a piece of candy from his pocket, Raz unwrapped it and popped the yellow candy into his mouth. "You want one?" He asked, pointing to his other pocket.

"No, thank you, I'm quite distracted now." Mark reached for the door and grabbed the handle, but before he opened the door, he heard Raz say one last thing before popping out of the room.

"Hope your light on your feet." Turning around once again, no one was there. He didn't know where the boy went, but for some reason, it infuriated him.

"I am all POWERFUL!" Mark began, "I did all of this. I am responsible for IT ALL!" Swinging the door open, he was met with the police holding guns to his head. "Oh God, not this again. How many of you are there?" Jenkins had his weapon at the Man while Finley put it away and pulled out his cuffs.

"Thank you for the confession, which makes my job easier." Finley began to walk towards Mark, but with a twist of his finger, Jenkins was now holding the gun to his head.

"I wouldn't come any closer, or your partner would blow his brains out." Pushing past the others, Andrew ran down the hall and tackled Jenkins causing his arms to fly out in front of him. The gun went off behind him, clipping Matt in the shoulder. Finley took the excitement and turned it into an opportunity, knocking Mark to the ground and cuffing his arms behind his back.

"Mr., you're under arrest."

Falling to the floor in the hallway, Hunter went to Matt's side. He was being pulled in two different directions, but without the contracts, he could do nothing to save William.

"We are the plagues," Hannah said once again; her eyes had become pure green and began to glow just like the crystal did when Darla was wearing it. William could feel his skin begin to burn, boils forming on his neck, and his eyesight began to waver.

"What's happening?" He asked in a raspy voice. Hannah's deep, gravelly voice emerged, sending chills down everyone's spine.

"I am Plague; I bring disease," William could feel his fingers necrotizing; his struggling had begun to take its toll.

Hunter ripped the bottom of his shirt and wrapped it tight around Matt's wound to keep the bleeding under control. Helping Matt to his feet, Hunter looked down the hall at what was happening.

"Drew, man, we need that briefcase, like now!!!"

Looking around the room, Drew didn't see the case anywhere, but then out of the corner of his eye, he saw something shiny on the desk across the room. Walking over to it, it became apparent that it was an old yellow candy wrapper, and the briefcase was under the desk. A smile crossed his face as he opened it, and there inside were the contracts.

"NO! You can't do that!" Mark screamed at Drew as he picked up the first contract and ripped it to shreds.

"AAAAAAAA!" The first plague screamed as he dropped William to the floor. The crystal around the boy's neck began to glow again, giving off an eerie illumination all around the room.

"What happened?" William asked as he got to his feet and joined the others in the hallway. William had recovered from the disease after the banishing of the first plague.

"I'm pretty sure Drew just banished the first plague," Hunter said, but the moment was short-lived when they began to feel the house move and shake, and Hannah walked out into the hallway; her eyes were now red, putting her hands up in front of them they were all pushed against the wall, her voice was now soft and sultry, that of a beautiful woman.

"I am famine, and I will devour your souls." The three men looked at each other and saw that they were wasting away right in front of their eyes.

"Any time today would be nice, Drew!" Hunter yelled. Picking up the second contract, Drew began to rip it to shreds, and the second plague was banished into the abyss. Andrew could hear Mark beginning to laugh; his laughter began to get louder and louder.

"What's so funny, Mr. Randolph? You lost." Drew said; Finley began to pick the man up from the floor. Jenkins, who had recovered from the blow, also had his gun on the suspect.

"Missing something?" Mark said with a smirk. Looking down into the case, he could see only one contract left. "It's either the darkness or the rising. My bet is the latter. You're screwed, Mr. Bower; you all are because you were on the wrong side of history, and I'm going to be the singular most powerful being on the planet."

"The moon is bleeding, Drew! Do your thing, and it's almost over." Mark let out another loud and ablations snort.

Hannah had walked up to Hunter, the others still pinned against the wall, her eyes as black as coal, and kissed him. His eyes also became black as night, and you could see the panic on his face.

"I'm blind! Drew, I'm BLIND!" Drew ran out into the hallway with the last contract and ripped it to shreds as he ran down the hallway. Hannah fell to her knees, and her breathing began to become labored. Drew cautioned past her and noticed that Hunter's eyes were returning to their natural color. Peeking out of the window, the moon had also begun to return to its natural shine.

"We have a problem." Drew began,

"What? What now?" Matt asked as they all began to get released from the wall.

"Mark took the last contract, and I'm sure it's a doozy because he was rambling and laughing and acting like a crazy person. The police officers are taking him to the police station now. So, there are two fewer people here to worry about." The four men looked over at the girl, who was regaining her posture; her eyes were now the bluest shade they had ever seen.

"I am the rise, the recreator of the dead, I am the puppeteer," Lifting her hands over her head, the men began to hear the sounds they only thought were possible in horror movies.

"Seriously," Hunter said as he scanned the hallway for weapons. "It had to be zombies?" The voice on the other side of Hannah laughed. It sounded like an old lady who had outlived her years; she began to float towards them, but that was the least of their worries as they all watched in horror at the lumbering creatures behind her.

First was Willow, then Father Hall, and then cautiously taking up the back of the group, was Keen.

"Keen," Matt said, and Drew could tell that he had grown fond of the man.

"I'm sorry, Matt." Drew looked around the hallway and vanished into the bedroom where Hannah had been sleeping.

"How do we find the contract?" Hunter asked with a stutter as the monstrous hoard began to lumber toward them, a look of hunger on their face. Willow's gurgling sounds bothered Matt the most; every time she would open her mouth, black ooze would roll down the hole where the bullet had gone in.

The three of them heard the breaking glass in the room. Glancing over to see what Drew was doing, they noticed that he had begun to tear the room apart, looking for the contract. He had broken the mirror on the wall to make a blade wrapping its end in a shirt he had found in the closet.

Hannah walked closer, looking at the three of them with her giant blue eyes. The closer she got, the more the crystal glowed, and William's eyes got wild with excitement.

"It's her!" He said, "She has the contract!"

"Were though, she's wearing a nightgown. I doubt it has pockets." Matt said, but Hunter spared no time; the ravenous lumbering meat bags were right at her heels. Running towards her, Hunter grabbed her twirling her around and putting her in a bear hug, but it exposed his arms to the zombies. Willow, the first to approach him, opened her mouth and bit down as hard as she could, ripping a large chunk of flesh from Hunter's forearm. Screaming in horror and pain, he fell to the floor, taking Hannah with him.

Pushing past the hoard, Keen lumbered forward, and Hunter knew that it would be the end for him, but in a surprise twist, Keen grabbed Willow's head and twisted it off like a bottle cap. Dropping it to the floor, he looked down at Hunter and Hannah. Then he looked at the paper that had slipped from the girl's gown.

"Is this what you're looking for?" The man asked, picking up the paper.

"Keen! You're okay!" Matt said, with happiness in his voice.

"I wouldn't say okay, but I'm alive." Father Hall was coming up behind Keen, but he spared no seconds and ripped the paper up, letting it fall to the floor. Standing like a statue, Father Hall made one last twitch before falling to the ground beside Keen.

Drew ran out of the room and swung the glass at Keen but was stopped by Matt.

"He's alive, and it's over." Hannah and Hunter got to their feet and Drew dropped the glass to check on Hunter's arm.

"I don't know how these things work. Am I going to turn now?"

"I highly doubt it, but I would check into getting a rabies shot." said the voice from the end of the hall at the top of the steps. The man looked over at Hunter; he had long black hair and was wearing blue jeans and a leather jacket with a white tee.

"Where did you come from?" Hunter asked. Hannah rubbed her eyes and looked over at the man. She smiled and ran over to him.

"I know him, and he's a friend. Raz, right?" Smiling over at the girl, he took her hand and nodded. "Is it time?" Again, he nodded at her, and she smiled, wrapping her arms around his neck.

Here they were again, standing in front of the door. Hannah, Hunter, William, Matthew, Andrew, and Raz.

"Are you sure this is what you want to do, Will?" Drew asked, crossing his arms and looking over at the boy thoughtfully.

"Yes, they will need me if what Raz says is true. Plus, there is nothing left here for me." Hugging Hannah, William handed the Crystal over to Raz, nodding at the man in solidarity. "You ready to go, Matt?" Matt shook his head.

"I can't believe I'm doing this, but at least I will have my best bro right there with me." Walking over to the door, just like before, Raz placed the crystal in its home, and the ground beneath them began to shake and tremble, and then the door opened. Without another word, the two boys walked through and into the abyss, but Hunter and Andrew thought they could hear Darla from the other side call out to William just as the door closed.

This time the door closed on itself, leaving the four of them standing at the mountain's base.

"What are we going to say to their parents? To Chairperson Howards?" Hunter asked as he picked up the Crystal and tried to hand it back to Raz, but he declined it.

"Once they walked through that portal, they no longer existed here," Raz said as they all began to walk back to the car.

"Then how come we remember?" Drew asked.

"That's our curse to bear because we witnessed them cross over. Oh, and even though it's just a suggestion, I would keep that necklace someplace safe. I have a feeling your gonna need it." Raz said with a mischievous grin.

"Thank you for keeping me company in the nothing while the Plagues had control. I might have gone insane otherwise. How will you get back to where you're from, Raz?" Looking over at Hannah, the man took her hand and smiled.

"It wasn't any trouble at all; that's where I do some of my best work. I have ways of popping up when I'm needed."

"What are you? Some interdimensional outer space explorer?" Hunter asked.

"Aren't we all?" Raz said, and with that, the three of them heard a little pop, and the weird man was gone.

"Well, what do we do now?" Hannah asked as they got back into the car. Starting the loud yellow hooptie up, Drew drove into the sunrise.

"I don't know, Hannah, but we've got it all under control by the looks of things."

Megan O'Dell Guilliams is a Franklin County native. Currently residing in Rocky Mount, Virginia, she lives with her husband Travis, two children Taylor and Devan, their Pomeranian Smokey, and the newest addition to the family, a little Chihuahua Pug lovingly nicknamed 'Burt'. When she's not writing young adult fiction, Megan enjoys painting original lowbrow art filling her house walls to the brim with colorful and imaginative works. She also enjoys spending time with her family, watching movies, and playing board games as well as going to the local park and walking the dogs.